THE GUNS OF STINGAREE

STINGAREE

A SHAWN STARBUCK WESTERN

THE GUNS OF STINGAREE

A SHAWN STARBUCK WESTERN

RAY HOGAN

Thorndike Press • Chivers Press
Thorndike, Maine USA   Bath, England

This Large Print edition is published by Thorndike Press, USA
and by Chivers Press, England.

Published in 2001 in the U.S. by arrangement with
Golden West Literary Agency.

Published in 2001 in the U.K. by arrangement with
Golden West Literary Agency.

U.S. Hardcover 0-7862-3140-8 (Western Series Edition)
U.K. Hardcover 0-7540-4441-6 (Chivers Large Print)
U.K. Softcover 0-7540-4442-4 (Camden Large Print)

The text of this Large Print edition is unabridged.
Other aspects of the book may vary from the original edition.

Set in 16 pt. Plantin by Susan Guthrie.

Printed in the United States on permanent paper.

British Library Cataloguing-in-Publication Data available

Library of Congress Cataloging-in-Publication Data

Hogan, Ray, 1908–
   The guns of Stingaree : a Shawn Starbuck Western /
by Ray Hogan.
     p. cm.
   ISBN 0-7862-3140-8 (lg. print : hc : alk. paper)
   1. Starbuck, Shawn (Fictitious character) — Fiction.
2. Large type books. I. Title.
PS3558.O3473 G83 2001
813'.54—dc21   00-053628

THE GUNS OF STINGAREE

A SHAWN STARBUCK WESTERN

CHAPTER 1

King Mallory halted on the Gila Valley's east ridge and threw his glance angrily down upon the ranch sprawled below. Boone Rafferty, the bull-headed sonofabitch, had turned him down for the last time! Big head thrust forward, his great bulk resting heavily in the saddle, he continued to study moodily the scatter of buildings, and then, as if suddenly remembering, he shifted his obsidian black eyes to the three Stingaree hired hands he'd brought with him and who had pulled up a respectful distance to his left.

"Get on back to the ranch," he snapped, and abruptly looked away.

Rafferty was a fool. He should have noticed that the men he'd brought along were just regular cowhands and not any of the hardcase bunch he, and others in the valley, referred to as Stingaree's Troubleshooters. That alone should have proved to Boone that he had come to make his final offer to buy in good faith. But Boone, damn him, hadn't seen that. He'd always been stupid, slow to grasp things; he'd gotten worse in these last few years, however. He certainly wasn't this bad when they were in California.

Hawking, Mallory spat into the loose shale at the base of a close-by talus. This finished it. He was through horsing around. If Rafferty couldn't be reasonable and sell out Arrowhead willingly, then he'd do it the hard way. Nobody yet had been able to withstand the Mallory drive to own the entire Gila Valley, to make it part of Stingaree — and a stubborn, dumb-witted, dockwalloper like Boone Rafferty wasn't going to be the first!

Boone would change his mind plenty quick after a couple of night visits from the Troubleshooters. Hell, the man didn't know how lucky he was! They'd been held off for over a year now while he tried to reason out a deal. Forcing Rafferty's hand wouldn't be the cinch it had been with all the others in the valley. Arrowhead was a big spread, and persuading Boone with Stingaree guns meant a young war with a lot of men throwing a lot of lead around. You'd think Rafferty could see that and come to terms, but no, the fool was flat-out refusing to sell.

Well, it wouldn't last long. Nobody bucked Stingaree for any length of time. Of course, he couldn't expect Arrowhead to

8

cave in fast, like most of the others. Rafferty would make a stand, string things out and get his men shot up, but it would come to the same end — Rafferty would finally sell and Arrowhead would become a part of Stingaree.

Brushing his hat to the back of his head, Mallory twisted about, looked off to the south where the wooded slopes slipped down to become the flats. A large, solidly built Tennessean with a will and a hand of iron, he sat erect on his horse, thick body and wide shoulders rigid in their carriage. Dark-haired, heavy-browed, with a hard line for a mouth, he was a picture of power and ruthlessness — a fact in which he gloried rather than denied.

He had come into the Gila Valley country a little more than ten years ago, bringing with him a wife, a son, a daughter, and plenty of money. Boone Rafferty had been with him, too, equipped equally with a sufficiency of cash — but no family. Together they had set to work building up ranches, Mallory starting his Stingaree spread in the south-center of the area, Rafferty laying out Arrowhead immediately to the north.

Beef was in demand in the eastern markets and they had done well, so well that King had soon felt the need to expand his holdings in order to produce more cattle. Boone had been content to stay as he was, rock along at the same even pace, having no ambition to grow and make more of his ranch.

While there had existed an undercurrent of unexplained tension between them from the day they arrived, they had more or less fallen out over that very question of respective growth — nothing serious at first, but a gradual drifting apart that steadily widened as Mallory went about the business of absorbing small ranches and homesteads that lay in his path.

The total and final rupture came abruptly and brought them to complete and conclusive odds. Mallory took over the holdings of a close friend of Rafferty's. It had not been an amicable transaction, and before it was consummated the Troubleshooters had to be sent in and hash made of the place. Boone then declared himself and told his one-time goldfield partner what he thought of his ambitions and the methods employed in their pursuit. King had laughed in his face and there the declining friendship that had begun in boyhood came to an irrevocable close.

What had been a coolness between them now bordered on hatred, and the only instances the two men had spoken to each other were on the three occasions during the past year or so when Mallory had approached Rafferty on the matter of selling out to him. Those conversations had been brief and to the point — Mallory stating his offer, Boone Rafferty giving his blunt refusal.

But now even the time for that was over. King, the desire burning more fiercely than ever within him, had to have Arrowhead not only because it would add another sixty thousand acres to the ninety he already owned, but also because, once it became his, the entire Gila Valley — except for four small outfits that would come to heel once they saw Boone Rafferty was out of it — would be Stingaree. He'd have the finest ranch in the Southwest, a veritable beef factory — one that undoubtedly would make the big Texas cattle barons squirm with envy.

Wiping at the sweat on his forehead, he jerked his hat into place and swung back up the slope, walking the bay gelding he'd chosen to ride that day at a slow, easy pace. There was a time when he first came into the Gila county when he would have enjoyed riding through the fresh, pine-scented high country, taking pleasure in the

11

haunting song of the wind blowing through the trees, the vivid splash of reds, purples, and yellows of flowers here and there blanketing a slope.

That had gone, too, along with a lot of other aesthetic nonsense, and now all was strict, unqualified practicality. He was a man caught up in the steel fingers of a surging need to be the most powerful, the most feared, and the most envied personage in the western part of the land. It wasn't to end there. Once that was attained, then he would turn to politics — Governor of the Territory, Representative in Congress, a big job in Washington. Hell, a man could do anything he set his mind to if he didn't let anything or anybody get in his way.

That was the secret. Never let sentiment or friendship become part of your way of life. Get what you want by whatever means necessary and don't worry about what comes later.

Later. . . . That did trouble him some — not the effect his actions might have on others, but the future of Stingaree once it reached the point toward which he was striving. Who would look after it, hang on to what he'd gained, fight off the wolves who would certainly close in and try to pull the mighty spread to pieces while he was away looking after other matters?

He couldn't figure on Jack, his son. He was about as worthless and no-account as they came, with no talent for anything other than tipping the bottle and hanging around Kottman's Saloon in town. He'd tried, Lord knows he'd tried to make a real man out of Jack, but it had been wasted effort. And Theodosia, his wife, and Christine, their daughter, being women, were of course out of the question.

Frank Price, his foreman? Frank was good at growing beef, there was no denying that, but it ended right there. He had no spunk, no get-up-and-go, and besides he was getting old. Rafe McCoskey, who sort of captained the Troubleshooters? He was good at his job, but he had no sense and he sure as hell couldn't be trusted. He'd bleed Stingaree dry in a year.

Mallory swore, again mopped at his brow. Prospects stopped there — and that was one hell of a note to think about! A man builds up a cattle empire second to none, has maybe forty or fifty hands working for him, and there wasn't a goddam one, including his own son, able to take over and run things for him. What was wrong with men nowadays? Either they had no sense or no guts, or they just plain didn't give a hoot about making something of themselves.

He'd held out hopes for Christine, at least for a time, thinking she'd meet some likely man, marry him, and thus provide a candidate for the job. Then he would have someone he could at least try to whip into his image, but somehow the girl had never met the right fellow. Once or twice she'd gotten herself all keened-up on some ordinary cowhand who amounted to nothing and he'd been forced to put an end to it.

He supposed he couldn't really blame her too much; she didn't get much of a chance to meet the right kind, and the years she'd spent back East attending some damned girl's school had been a waste insofar as getting a husband was concerned, too. The sort of la-de-da jaspers she'd run into back there usually didn't know a stirrup from a cantle, much less have the ability to take over the running of a spread like Stingaree — not even if he spent a hundred years teaching them the tricks.

But he reckoned she was still his best bet. Maybe it would be smart to send her and Theodosia up to Denver, let them put up in one of the big hotels and live there for a few months. Could be she'd get acquainted with some fellow who amounted to more than a row of pins. It was just about his last hope

14

and he guessed he'd better do it right away. He intended to lead McCoskey and his gunnies in the first raid upon Rafferty's that night, now that he knew there was no possibility of making a peaceable deal. With a little luck he'd have Arrowhead under the Stingaree brand and the other hold-outs whipped into line in short order, and he'd be free to start thinking about a political future, except for someone to —

Abruptly King Mallory reined in the bay. A deep frown puckered his brow as he fell to stroking the full mustache that covered his upper lip. By God, maybe he was overlooking a good bet.

That new puncher he'd hired a couple of weeks ago, the one who'd come there looking for his brother. Starbuck, he'd said his name was. He'd thought then the jasper had possibilities, but somehow it had slipped out of his mind. Young, tough, fast as hell with that gun he wore on his left hip. Good with it, too; a couple of days after he'd gone to work he'd seen the fellow cut the head off a rattler at least fifty feet away and do it so quick you could hardly see him at it. Had good cow sense, as well. Frank Price was already shifting some of the more important jobs onto his shoulders.

Come to think of it, he'd be a fine prospect for Christine — and he'd be a goddam good man to head up the Troubleshooters. That could be a sort of testing ground, a way of letting him prove himself. McCoskey wouldn't like it, but the hell with him. All you could say for Rafe was that he was good with a gun — nothing else. He was ready to get rid of him, anyway.

Come to think of it, this Starbuck seemed to have it all. He'd call him in soon as he got in off the range, have a talk. The kind of a deal he was prepared to offer him, assuming he measured up, was one no man in his right mind could turn down.

(HAPTER 2

This was where, one day, he'd like to have his own ranch, Starbuck thought as he rode slowly through the cedars and oak brush.

The Gila Valley, fifty miles long, almost thirty wide at its extreme, was the promised land — one of lush, green grass, broadly spreading trees, and ample, year-round water. Nestled in the hollow of tall, pine-clad mountains, it was well shielded from the icy blasts that occasionally roared in from the north during the snow months, and from the hot, scorching winds that came from the desert to the west in the summer.

But that day when he could think of settling down, of starting his own spread, was likely far off. First Ben must be found, for only then could the estate of their father, Hiram, be settled and his share of the money become available for the realization of the dream.

Eventually, however, the long, often discouraging search he was conducting for his brother would end, and he'd then be able to think of the future. He could only hope it would not come too late, that he would still feel the urge to have his own ranch, build a spread such as the man he was now working for, King Mallory, had done.

Not that he could ever expect to possess a place such as Stingaree — or even want one so extensive. It had taken more thousands of dollars than he would ever see to come up with such a ranch. But he'd have enough to provide all he'd want.

A man wouldn't need any great amount of land in the Gila Valley, grazing being what it was. Twenty, twenty-five thousand acres would do fine. It was unlike the more barren mesa range where a rancher could figure on only one or two steers pasturing on twenty acres; here a man could raise at least eight or perhaps ten to the acre!

Starbuck grinned, brushed at his sun- and wind-browned face. What the hell was he mooncalfing about? With Ben somewhere off in the dim yonder, chimerical as fox fire and seemingly as impossible to lay hands on as a summer cloud, he had about as much chance of starting a ranch in the Gila as he did of flying! By the time he found his brother and had money enough to begin, the valley would be locked up tight as a drum by men like Stingaree's King Mallory and Arrowhead's Boone Rafferty, along

18

with a few others who knew a good thing when they saw it.

But it was where he'd like to be and he couldn't help dreaming about it. There were other places just as good, he supposed, although he couldn't exactly recall them at the moment. When he was finally able, he guessed he'd be able to locate a similar valley somewhere — but he'd do that only after he was certain there was no land left in the Gila.

Drawing the sorrel he was riding to a stop, he eased forward on the saddle to rest his leg muscles. He'd been riding steadily since shortly after daybreak, looking for strays. Price, Stingaree's ramrod, had sent him out early with another of the hands, Emmett Stark, to spend the day brushpopping. He hadn't seen Emmett for three or four hours, reckoned he was somewhere on the broad slope to the east where piñon and mountain mahogany grew thick.

It had been Stark's idea to split up, he taking the upper regions while Starbuck worked the foot of the grade. The plan had proven a success. Between them they had choused out over a dozen fat steers along with several cows with calves. A range could have too much growth on it, he decided; it made for a lot of strays and that called for plenty of extra work.

But Mallory had a large supply of hired hands around to do the job. He'd never really met the rancher face to face yet, had only seen him around a few times — a big-bellied, hard-talking, rough-edged man who made his presence felt by everyone. He had a son, Jack, who appeared to have no duties other than loafing, palling around with the gunslingers that were on the pay-roll, and riding back and forth to Parsonville, the settlement ten or twelve miles east. He also had a wife and daughter who were always kept well in the back-ground, as if they counted for nothing.

Which, if he was to do any judging of Mallory by the men of similar stripe he'd met in the past, was exactly the way of it. Only one person would count in King Mallory's life and that was King Mallory.

Starbuck didn't particularly like the type, but the day he'd ridden into Stingaree looking for signs of Ben as well as a job and Frank Price had offered him a place on the crew at better than usual wages, he'd taken it. He hadn't known about King Mallory then, would not have permitted it to bother him if he had. Every man had the right to be himself, and sixty a month was good pay — so good in fact that if he stuck around until the first of the year he'd have enough cash stashed away in his poke to quit and resume the hunt for Ben without being forced to halt it again soon.

That had been the drawback all along, the factor that was causing the search for Ben to run on so interminably. The will old Hiram had left specified that he must find his older brother and bring him back to Muskingum, in Ohio, and to the lawyer who was administering the estate.

What Hiram Starbuck neglected to do was supply any funds for the search, so it was a matter of drifting about, pursuing the quest until he ran out of cash, then finding a job for a while to rebuild his finances. At sixty a month, though, instead of the usual thirty or forty, he'd put himself in good shape very fast.

Cupping a hand to shield his eyes, Starbuck looked ahead for Emmett. They should start working back toward the ranch. The stock they had driven out of the brush and pointed for the main herd grazing farther to the west likely had stopped by now and were beginning to drift. They should get behind them, keep them moving in the right direction.

There was no sign of his partner. Evidently he was farther along on the slope

21

than expected. Starbuck roweled the sorrel lightly, continued on, weaving in and out of the springy growth patiently. Steers were expert at hiding in brush, and a man could pass one by with ease if he didn't keep a sharp watch.

Motion to his left brought Starbuck around quickly. A gray and brown old longhorn, head slung low, legs spread, was considering him with wall-eyed interest. Starbuck wheeled swiftly, cut the gelding in behind the steer, and using his doubled rope as a whip, laid a lash upon the animal's rump.

The steer lunged forward, setting up a noisy crackling of brush as he rushed through and headed back for the range at a lope. *Eighteen in all,* Starbuck thought, resuming his slow pace along the foot of the slope. Frank Price had been right; there was quite a bit of beef hiding out in the fringes of the ranch.

He wondered about Price. That he was a good foreman and knew his business was evident, but there appeared to be something bothering him, an uncertainty of some kind, as if he mistrusted his own abilities and feared for his job. Starbuck had heard rumors that Mallory was plenty hard on him, just as he'd heard other rumors to the effect that the rancher was out to take over the entire Gila Valley, but he passed such off as only idle talk.

It could be true where Price was concerned, however. Up in years, the man could be worried about losing his place at Stingaree all right, and the possibility was turning him inward and bringing about a sort of caution.

Undoubtedly, Mallory would recognize the fear and make the most of it. His kind usually took such advantage, finding some sort of joy in making the man concerned miserable. He hoped he'd not fall under the attention of the rancher and come in for a lot of unwarranted rawhiding and hoorawing. He'd stand and take his licks if he did something wrong, but just to be the object of another man's temper whim for no good reason was something else. As much as he'd like to hang onto the job, he'd throw it back into King Mallory's face if it ever came to such. He needed work, sure, but not at the expense of his own self-respect.

It was strange how a lot of money affected some men, and Starbuck fell to wondering if Mallory had always been the sort he evidently was now. Caleb Fain, the crippled old bronc stomper who was Stingaree's head wrangler and had been around for a long time, said Mallory had gotten his start in forty-nine during the California gold rush. He'd gone there with Boone Rafferty, the owner of the Arrowhead ranch to the north. They'd been boyhood friends back somewhere in Tennessee, had grown up together, and were more or less partners in the venture to California.

They'd hit it rich and returned to Tennessee, then later had moved west, settling eventually side by side in the Gila Valley and going into the cattle business. Somewhere along the line something had happened to end their friendship, and now it was said they rarely if ever spoke to each other. What it was that brought them to a parting Caleb didn't know, but he suspected it had something to do with the way Mallory had done business with others in the area.

Caleb said something else, too — that King wasn't really Mallory's given name. The old rider said it was all a secret, and those who knew of it took pains never to mention it, but it had been Horatio Mallory at the start; the rancher had changed it after he had settled in the valley and begun to get big ideas about himself.

Starbuck reckoned that was as good a key to the man's inner self as anything and let it

go at that. Mallory could call himself whatever he wished; all that was important was
that he offered good wages for a job done
and could be depended upon to pay them at
the end of every month.

Movement again at the edge of a small
cluster of trees drew Starbuck's attention. . . . More strays — no, it was a horse, a
saddled and bridled one, not one of the
older mounts turned loose to roam free over
the range. Concern suddenly gripped
Starbuck as he drew nearer and was furnished a better look. It was the black that
Emmett Stark had been riding. The animal
was just beyond a bulge of rocks on the
slope, grazing indifferently on the thick
grass.

Starbuck spurred forward. Emmett evidently had been thrown, was lying hurt
somewhere nearby. He rounded the
shoulder of rocks, drew up short. Stark and
Mallory's daughter, arms about each other,
were standing at the fringe of the trees. A
spotted pony, undoubtedly the girl's, was a
short distance beyond them. At Starbuck's
sudden appearance, the pair broke apart,
wheeled to face him.

It was a bad situation. King Mallory's
anger would reach no limit if he knew his
daughter was carrying on with an ordinary

cowhand. As for Stark, he'd be fortunate if losing his job was all that happened to him. The rancher might hold his female offspring in low esteem insofar as family importance was concerned, but perversely, he'd not countenance her marrying beneath what he'd determined as the proper level.

But it was none of his business, Starbuck knew, and immediately cut the sorrel about and started a hasty retreat. In that same moment Emmett's voice checked him.

"Shawn — hold up!"

CHAPTER 3

Starbuck rode reluctantly toward the pair. He would prefer to have no part in any clandestine affair involving King Mallory's daughter and Stark — or anyone else for that matter — but he was trapped.

"Want to explain," Emmett said hesitantly.

"No need," Starbuck replied, drawing to a halt. "I —"

"Are you going to tell Papa?" the girl broke in anxiously. There was genuine fear in her eyes.

Shawn shrugged. "No business of mine. Doubt if I'll ever be doing any talking to him, and if I did, it sure wouldn't be about you two."

"Is that a promise?" she persisted.

Starbuck made no reply. Emmett Stark smiled apologetically. "You've got to excuse Christine," he said. "Plenty around here who'd jump at the chance to go tattling to her pa. They'd figure it'd put them in good with him."

"Doesn't include me. . . . That being the case, seems to me you're taking a long chance, meeting out like this."

"Only choice we've got," Stark said. "And we've been lucky so far. Anyway, far as I'm concerned, it's worth it."

Starbuck allowed his glance to rest on the girl. It was the first time he'd seen her at close range. Small, about his own early-twenty age, she was well-shaped, had chestnut-brown hair and medium-blue eyes.

"Can understand that," he murmured.

Christine Mallory smiled, looked away. Stark grinned also, said jokingly, "Now, don't you go getting no ideas!"

"Wouldn't think of it. How long have you two been courting?"

"Four, almost five months," the girl said.

"And your family's still in the dark about it?" The expression on the girl's face stiffened, reflected the intense feeling she had for her father. "Papa is — and so's Jack. Mother knows, or maybe guesses, but she won't say anything."

"It's kind of bad," Stark said, shaking his head. "Expect you figure I've got a lot of gall making up to the boss's daughter, me not being much of anything."

"That's not true!" Christine exclaimed. "You could be plenty if you only had the chance."

Emmett Stark, a tall, pale-eyed man with

a thick shock of light hair, stirred helplessly. "Something I reckon I'll never get around here. Most I can look for on this place is cowhand wages."

"We could leave," the girl said in a hopeful voice.

Stark frowned. "Now, we've been all through that before. I won't hear of it."

Christine sighed. "Then all we can do is make the best of things the way they are." She paused, looked off beyond the trees. "I'll have to be getting back. It's not safe to be gone too long."

She turned away at once, started slowly toward the spotted pony. As Stark turned to follow he threw a glance over his shoulder at Shawn.

"Be coming right away —"

Starbuck nodded, wheeled the sorrel about and moved to the far side of the rocks, halted. Shortly, Stark, astride his horse, appeared. His lean features were glum.

"Sure wish I could do something about her and me. Way it stacks up I'm same as hog-tied."

They moved out together, side by side, heading across the range. Christine, Starbuck supposed, was circling wide to approach the ranchhouse from a different direction.

"Stingaree's not the only place where a man can find work."

"Know that," Emmett replied, "but the pay won't be no good — lower'n I'm getting here, probably, and that ain't enough for a man to support a wife on — 'specially one like Chris. She won't agree. She'd pull out with me right now if I'd say the word, but I just can't see dragging her down to that kind of living. She's used to plenty."

"Probably to more than any man she could marry will be able to give her at the start," Starbuck said. "Don't know much about things like that but it always seems to me that the couples having the toughest going in the beginning pan out to be the happiest."

Emmett sleeved sweat from his face. Ahead, a half dozen of the steers they'd earlier driven out of the brush had halted to graze. Stark swept off his hat and waving it above his head spurred toward the animals. They broke into a run, pounding off across the grassy flat.

"Expect that's the truth," he said, swinging back to Starbuck's side. "You ever been married?"

"Nope. Just never had time."

Emmett grinned. "I'm betting the real answer to that is you've never met the right woman."

"No, that's not the way of it. I've come across a few that sort of got to me, set me to thinking about a place of my own — then I'd come to and ride on. Had to."

"Because of this brother you're looking for?"

"That's it. No point in me figuring a life for myself until I've found him and gotten Pa's business all settled."

"Heard you telling Caleb about it the other night. Something about an estate."

"My pa's. Quite a bit of money being held in a bank until I can find Ben. Then we get our share. Be more than enough to set me up on my own ranch."

Emmett nodded. "Can savvy why you won't give up your looking. Why'd your brother run off in the first place?"

"He and Pa had a falling out. We lived on a farm in Ohio. Place near the Muskingum River. Pa'd told Ben to do some chores. He forgot. They had a big row and Ben pulled out. Said he'd never come back and that he was going to change his name so's nobody'd ever know he was related."

"He do that?"

"Yes. Learned for sure only a while back. Calls himself Damon Friend now. You ever hear of a man by that name?"

"Nope. Starbuck, either. There only the

two of you in the family — kids, I mean?"

"Ben and me, that's all. Like as not we'd still be living back there on the farm if my mother hadn't died. She was a fine woman and my pa thought more of her than anything else in the world — including Heaven. When she died one winter from lung fever, he changed plenty. They were a couple who had it hard to start with and built themselves a fine life."

"She some rich man's daughter?"

"No, just ordinary folks. She was a schoolteacher. Worked with the Indians some."

Stark nodded in satisfaction. "Had a hunch that name of yours was Indian. Comes from Shawnee, don't it?"

"Right. It was the Shawnee people she was around. Liked the sound of the word, I guess, and made it into a name for me when I came along."

Emmett heaved a deep sigh. "Sure do wish Christine's folks was like others — leastwise her pa." The puncher's jaw hardened. "Don't like saying it, but he's a mean, ornery sonofabitch and I've got myself hating him just like his whole family does — along with everybody else in the country. You ever come across a man like him that couldn't name himself one friend in the whole world?"

"Can't say as I have."

"Well, you sure have now, and if you have any truck with him, you'll find yourself getting in line with the rest of us haters."

"Don't ever expect to get that close to him."

"Maybe not," Stark said, disconsolately. "Reckon you don't have to, either. You got something to look forward to. One of these days you'll find your brother and get your share of all that money your pa stashed away. Then you can find the woman you want and settle down to a fine life. Me — I've got nothing ahead."

"Nothing but a lot of years, and you're strong and a good man with cattle. Maybe the smart thing for you to do is make a place for yourself right here on Stingaree."

Emmett reined in abruptly, stared at Shawn. "You plumb loco or something?"

"Don't think so. Seems to me you're missing a bet in not trying to make a score with Mallory. Expect he's always looking for good men he can depend on and that know the business."

Stark's face was still a startled blank. "Me talk to King Mallory — ask him —"

Shawn shrugged. "That would be what I'd do if I had your problem. . . . He can't do anything but say no, and if he knew he was talking to the man who was going to be his son-in-law —"

"My God!" Emmett exploded. "You think I'd ever mention that to him?"

"Why not?"

The puncher settled back, put his horse into motion again with a light flick of the reins. "Yeh, why not?" he muttered. "Things couldn't get no worse, and if he run me off the place like as not it'd be better for Chris and me both."

"Might not work out that way. Got a hunch Mrs. Mallory'd be for anything her daughter wants. That would put her on your side."

"Mallory'd pay no mind to her. Never does. Chris told me he treats her like she wasn't even around — or alive. Fine woman, too, I think."

"Probably has her say when something important enough comes along."

Emmett snorted. "Can tell you ain't been in the Gila for long. King Mallory don't listen to nobody. It's the other way — folks listen to him whether they want to or not."

Stark paused, scrubbed agitatedly at the stubble on his chin. "You for sure think I ought to talk to him?"

"Like I said, if I was in your boots, I would."

"What'd I say?"

"Tell him you want a better job. Place could use another ramrod, a sort of an assistant to Frank Price. Or maybe you could take on the chore of buying and selling cattle for him."

"Does that himself."

"Means nothing. There's a chance he'd like to turn the job over to somebody else, somebody that knows cattle. Expect Jack would be doing it for him if he could be depended upon."

Emmett spat. "He ain't no good for anything."

"Just where you might fit in — become the son that Jack's not. If you don't want to say anything about you and Christine yet, let it pass. Get him to give you a chance to prove yourself, then after you have, it'll be easy to talk to him about his daughter. You work out good for him, he'll probably welcome the idea of having you in the family."

"Beginning to think maybe you're right," the puncher said thoughtfully. "See first if I can't get him to give me a bigger job, then work like hell so's he'll see I'm all right."

Starbuck glanced ahead. They were approaching the ranch. He could see the roofs of the sheds and a portion of the lower corral beyond the line of brush and trees that surrounded the place. Moments later, as they broke into the open, the yard came into view.

Fifteen or twenty members of the crew were gathered in front of the bunkhouse. Slightly apart from them, Frank Price faced King Mallory, and from the appearance of the two some sort of heated discussion was underway with Mallory doing most of the talking.

"Could be you'll get your chance to proposition the boss right away," Shawn said. "If it'll help any, I'm willing to stand beside you, put in my penny's worth."

Emmett swallowed hard. "Obliged," he mumbled, eyes fastened on the rancher, "but I ain't so sure now I can do it."

CHAPTER 4

They rode into the yard and halted at the first of the corrals. Dismounting, they began to strip the gear off their mounts, conscious as they did of the angry rise and fall of Mallory's strident voice.

"He's sure on the prod about something," Stark muttered as they turned to cross the hardpack and join the rest of the crew.

Shawn made no reply. It appeared to be one of Mallory's general meetings, but he seemed to be addressing his scathing remarks to Price, who stood silent, hands behind his back, face tipped down. Just beyond the rancher, Starbuck noted Jack Mallory and the dozen or so hardcases who liked to be called Stingaree's Troubleshooters. More or less led by a swaggering gunslinger named Rafe McCoskey, they were a collection of saloon bums and outlaws, most of whom likely were wanted by the law. Evidently being in the employ of King Mallory gave them immunity.

The rancher paused as Starbuck and Emmett Stark moved into the assemblage. He gave them a sharp, irritated scrutiny with his agate-hard eyes.

"You're late showing up," he snapped. "Where the hell you been?"

Shawn felt the hair along his neck prickle with anger. "Working. Looking for strays," he said coldly.

"You was told I'd be here to do some talking at five o'clock. When I say five o'clock that's what I mean."

Starbuck frowned, glanced at Emmett. No one had given the word to them. It would have been Frank Price's responsibility. Evidently it had slipped his mind. Stark opened his mouth to explain but Shawn shook his head warningly. Nothing would be gained by putting the blame on the foreman's shoulders. But King Mallow was a step ahead of him.

"Can see you didn't know nothing about it," he said and swung back to Price. "You forget to tell them, Frank? That it?"

The ramrod stirred. "Rode out early — before I got the chance," he said lamely.

"The hell! Told you last night. Why didn't you pass the word to them then? Expect the truth is you just plain forgot. You're getting old, mister, too old for the job. Looks like I'm going to have to make some changes."

Caleb Fain eased in beside Starbuck.

Shifting the cud of tobacco in his mouth, he spat. "Mallory's been threatening Frank like that for nigh onto a year now. He's going to do it one of these days."

"Price ought to tell him to go right ahead."

The old wrangler looked closely at Shawn. "You're youngster enough to say something dumb like that. Fellow gets old as Frank, and me, he has to walk mighty easy."

"You take it off him if you were the ramrod and he was always cutting the ground out from under you in front of your men?"

Caleb spat a second stream of brown juice into the dust, cocked his head to one side. He was a small, craggy-faced, balding man with twisted, bowed legs but arms and shoulders developed far beyond normal by his years of experience in breaking wild horses.

"Well now, since you're asking, there's a powerful lot of difference 'twixt Frank and me. I ain't got no old woman and kids to worry about."

Mallory was talking, once more speaking to the crew as a whole. "I'm laying down the law here and now," he boomed. "I find any more of my steers stuck in that slough, dying, I'm cleaning out the whole damn bunch of you!"

McCoskey, hunched on his heels, said something aside to Jack. The younger Mallory laughed, made an answer. King flashed them a hard glance and both sobered.

"Funny to them," Caleb muttered, "but then I reckon they ain't got nothing to be bothered about. Jack's set for life and Rafe's got hisself a job that don't call for no sweating and pays good." Fain paused, dropped his voice even lower. "A man'd think King would put a stop to the boy hanging around Rafe, aping him, trying to be like him, the way he does. I figure Jack could turn into a pretty fair man was he to quit listening to Rafe and his pa'd treat him like a son."

"Might help some, too, was he to get his snoot out of a whiskey bottle," Stark commented drily.

"For a fact, but I reckon that's sort of a hiding place for him. Was a time when he tried making up to his pa and getting along, but that there King, he's mean as an old range bull with a passel of yearling heifers. Ain't nobody ever gets close to him."

Emmett Stark groaned softly. "He always that way?"

40

"Day and night — and he's been like that ever since I been on the place, and I been here since this here ranch was begun."

Mallory was still speaking, his big voice droning on and on. Price still stood with hands locked behind him, head bowed. The riders were giving Mallory their attention, but few, if any, were hearing the words with which he was lashing them. That such meetings were not uncommon had become evident to Shawn, although this was the first he had endured.

". . . Another thing. I'm getting goddam tired of the loafing I see going on. Happens I pay more wages than anybody else in the country. I expect more for that. I want every man working for me on the job at daylight and not back here standing around and looking to eat until after dark.

"Same goes for the ones on night herding. I ain't paying nobody to set around in the shade or lay around in the bunkhouse playing cards or shooting the bull. I'm paying you to herd cattle, keep after the strays, and clean out the water holes when they need it —"

Rafe McCoskey again made a remark at low voice and once more Jack Mallory laughed. The rancher whirled furiously upon his son.

"Dammit, what I'm saying ain't meant to be no joke! Was you having even half sense you'd see that and be paying some mind. Pity you ain't the man I'd hoped you'd be, then it could be you here looking out for the place instead of me having to do it, but no, you had to turn out about as useless as tits on a boar!

"Now, why don't you go find yourself a corner and suck on your bottle for a spell — get clean out of my sight. Same goes for you, Rafe. You ain't got no call being here. What I'm saying don't concern you even if you had sense enough to understand. . . . Take your bunch and light out."

The gunman drew himself upright slowly. His eyes narrowed and a scowl covered his features. For a long moment he glared hotly at the rancher; then as Jack plucked at his arm, he turned and moved off, the others of his gang falling in behind him.

"King sure is laying it on today," Caleb Fain said, wagging his head. "Been quite a spell since I've seen him this here worked up. Must be something sticking in his craw slantwise."

"Heard Emil Crane say he was over talking to Rafferty today," the rider behind the old wrangler said quietly. "He took Emil and a couple other boys with him. Could be that's it."

"Ain't no doubting," Caleb said decisively. "Boone prob'ly told him to go to hell same as he's done before. And somebody doing that sure riles old King."

"What's he want from Rafferty?" Starbuck wondered.

"His ranch — Arrowhead — that's all. Been trying to buy him out. Boone ain't selling."

"What's he want more land for? Not using all he's got now."

Fain grunted. "Hell, the whole country ain't going to be big enough for him!"

Shawn nodded his understanding. He'd run into the type before — men who owned more than they needed but were driven by some relentless force to possess even more. It was like a virulent, rampaging disease.

"Will he drop it now or you figure he'll keep on trying?"

Caleb swapped cheeks with his cud. "Arrowhead's big, so I ain't sure what King'll do. Always before he got what he took the notion to have, one way or another. This here place ain't always been this big. They's about a half dozen other ranches and homesteads King got his hands on that went into making it the size it is.

"But maybe, just maybe, the pirating'll end here. Rafferty and Arrowhead ain't no little two-bit outfit that'll give in the minute Rafe McCoskey and his bunch starts cracking down on it. Boone's kind of slow-moving but he'll fight — and King knows that. Ought to. They was plenty close friends for a long time."

"Heard that. They fall out over Mallory wanting Rafferty's ranch?"

"No, was a time before King got that in his head. I don't rightly know what —"

"You — Starbuck!"

At the sound of his name being called Shawn glanced up to Mallory. "Yeh?"

"Want to see you in my office — right away."

CHAPTER 5

Starbuck, surprised and puzzled, watched Mallory stride toward the room off the south end of the main house that served as an office. About him a heavy silence had fallen over the Stingaree riders, and he could feel their eyes, filled with suspicion, dwelling upon him.

From somewhere in the crowd a drawling voice inquired: "What's going on, Starbuck? You working kind of special for the boss — spying on us, maybe?"

Shawn made no answer. Emmett Stark caught at his arm. "You got a notion what he's wanting?"

"No, and I guess there's only one way to find out," Starbuck said and started across the yard.

Halfway he met Frank Price's direct, almost accusing gaze, realized what was running through the foreman's mind. Smiling faintly, he shook his head to reassure the older man, and continued on.

Mallory was seated behind a massive, Mexican hand-carved desk when Shawn halted in the doorway. The office was large.

Pictures and mounted heads of several deer, antelope, and buffalo hung on the walls. Immediately back of the rancher was a large calendar advertising HOLT'S LIGHTNING-FAST HAY KNIFE. A second chair placed in front of the desk was the only other piece of furniture in the room.

"Set yourself," Mallory said genially, motioning with his big hand. "We got some mighty important talking to do."

Starbuck crossed to the chair, spurs jingling, heels clacking noisily on the board floor, and sat down. If the rancher had called him in to offer Frank Price's job as ramrod for Stingaree, he'd be wasting his breath.

"You interested in making yourself a pile of money and fixing yourself up for life?" the rancher began, leaning back in his leather-covered swivel chair. "Course you are," he added before Shawn could reply. "Man'd be loco if he said no to that."

"Depends," Starbuck finally managed to say.

"Sure, sure," Mallory said, bobbing. He gave what passed for a smile, stroked his full mustache thoughtfully.

"Don't know exactly how I ought to put this, you being new around here, and not knowing much about the setup. Expect I

46

best start back a ways, but first off, let me ask you this — you like working on Stingaree?"

"Job's a job."

"Except this'n with me pays better." The rancher paused, studied Shawn for a long moment, and then as if suddenly realizing something, said, "Guess I know what's digging at you — that little session I had out there with Price and the boys. Well, it wasn't meant for you and some of the others that've been doing a good job.

"Have to jump right square in the middle of most of them every once in awhile. Cowhands are lazy, sort of runs with the breed, and if I don't raise hell with them now and then, nothing'd ever get done around here. Price don't seem able to get much out of them anymore."

"Not hard to see why — you going over his head, chewing him out in front of everybody. Doesn't leave him with much to work with."

Mallory's jaw tightened as quick anger swept through him. "Best you leave that to me," he said coolly. "I didn't build this ranch into the biggest and best in the Territory by pussyfooting around. I say what's needful and to hell with whose toes get tromped on. But that ain't why you're here."

47

Starbuck shrugged. "If it's Price's job you're aiming to offer me —"

"Not that a'tall! Going to have to let Frank go one of these days, that's for sure. Just too old to handle the work. But that's not it. What I'm figuring is a bigger job.

"Now, it's taken me a mighty long time to put Stingaree where it is. Started out with less than sixty thousand acres. Got close to ninety now, and I'm not done yet. When I get through Stingaree'll cover at least a hundred and fifty thousand acres — and that means the whole Gila Valley far as good grass range is concerned. Actually, Stingaree'll *be* the Gila Valley. That make you swallow a mite?"

Starbuck smiled. "Makes me wonder what you'll do with all that land."

"Make use of it, that's what. Every square foot. More grass means more cattle, and more cattle means more beef I can market. When I get set the way I'm aiming to, Stingaree'll be the country's main supply point for beef. Not even them big Texas outfits'll be able to match me.

"Some of them may claim more acreage but it's poor range, not worth much. Different here. Every bit of my ground's deep in grass and perfect when it comes to fattening steers. . . . You had a chance to look the place over yet?"

"Most of it. Some of your north range I haven't seen yet."

Mallory leaned forward. "Ain't I telling you the truth? You ever seen better country?"

"Can't say as I have. Was thinking that one day I'd like to own a ranch around here."

King Mallory rocked back. His lips were drawn into that same cynical smile as he shook his head. "You and every other galoot that rides through here — only it'll never happen! There ain't no land available. I own just about all of it right now, and what I don't, I soon will. Now, that's what I want to talk to you about — helping me get the part that ain't already mine."

Shawn recalled the comments of Caleb Fain and others. "Arrowhead?"

"Yessir, Rafferty's Arrowhead, for one. Then there's three others: old man Handleman's two-bit outfit the other side of him, Huckaby, a homesteader southeast of me, and Dave Lockridge, another squatter to the west. I get them out, the Gila's mine."

"None of them willing to sell?"

Mallory shook his head. "Rafferty's the key. He sells, they sell. He sets there, stubborn as a mule like he's doing now, they'll

49

set tight, too. Of course I could go right ahead, deal with them and pay no mind to Rafferty, but was he to change his thinking, the rest would come easy, save a lot of hard work — and trouble."

"And bullets," Shawn finished, drily.

Again the rancher looked closely at him. "You saying something like that's got me wondering a bit," he said after a time. "But I still figure I'm right. You've got the looks of a man that's been around. Act like it, too, and that's what I'm looking for — somebody that can handle himself right along with handling others and do a top job for me.

"Right now there ain't nobody on the place, save maybe you, that I calculate's worth the powder it'd take to blow him to hell. All just hired hands. Lazy, shiftless, and without a brain in their heads. I'm including my own son in the lineup. Could be, because he is my own flesh and blood, that I think he's worse than any of them, but it don't matter. I don't count him in on nothing, and you won't have to, either. If it wasn't for his ma, I'd've run him off a long time ago.

"Now, the job I'm offering you is this: I'm needing a smart man with plenty of guts and know-how to help me clean up the rest of the valley. I'm through fooling around with Boone Rafferty. I'm going to make him come to terms, same as I had to do some of the others. That done, then I'll crack down on Handleman and them two squatters, get them out of the way.

"I aim to take McCoskey and the Troubleshooters, pay a little call on Rafferty tonight. Probably burn down his barn, a few sheds, whatever else is handy. That'll give him a sample of what's coming to him if he still figures to just set there on his ass and thumb his nose at me.

"But he'll change, once he sees I mean business. Hell, he ain't got no reason to hold out. He's got no family and he don't need money. Just being bullheaded, that's all, but a little rough handling will make him see the light.

"Here's my proposition. I want you to take over my boys — the Troubleshooters — and do their thinking for them. Sure, I've got Rafe McCoskey, but what good sense he's got you could put on the end of a pin. You'd be the head of the bunch. I'd tell you what I wanted done, you'd saddle them up and go do it.

"First job'd be Rafferty's. You get him agreeing to sell out to me, then you'd go to work on Handleman. After he's took care of you'd only have the two nesters.

"Your pay'll be a hundred a month, which is pretty good wages — but that ain't all of it. You work hard at the job and get them four ready to sell out within the next couple of months and you've got an extra five-hundred-dollar bonus. You can keep it yourself or split it with your boys. I'll leave it up to you and say nothing about it either way you go. How's that sound?"

Starbuck had listened in silence, his square, stolid features revealing nothing of his inner thoughts. He stirred, said, "Why'd you pick me?"

"Thought I'd made that clear. Seen you use that gun you're wearing. Heard about how you beat hell out of that puncher the other day for saying something you didn't cotton to — and I just plain like the way you handle yourself. Anyways, I ain't through yet.

"Things work out right, and you showing up like I figure you will, then I've got something else in mind. Like for you to start taking over Stingaree, do a few of the chores I'm having to look after. Ain't decided yet what the wages would be, but we'd come to some figure that'd suit us both."

Mallory paused. Sweat had gathered on his face, and taking a bandana from a hip pocket, he mopped his features impatiently. Out in the yard, now filling steadily with darkness, one of the hands shouted to another and shortly the sound of a horse trotting across the sun-baked ground echoed hollowly inside the office.

"Getting late," the rancher murmured, putting away the bandana. Reaching out, he slid the big brass lamp standing on the desk forward. Firing a match with a thumbnail, he raised the chimney and set the wick to burning. As the soft, yellow glow flooded the room, he nodded crisply to Starbuck.

"Well, I've done my talking. What's your answer?"

Shawn rose slowly. To make almost a thousand dollars within the next few months would mean much to him. It would put an end to interrupting his search for Ben and taking a job to replenish finances for a year, even longer. He could replace some of his worn gear, treat himself to some new clothing. And if he wanted to hang around longer, accept the bigger job King Mallory had mentioned, he could build his stake even larger. It was a tempting offer insofar as the pay was concerned, but he shook his head.

"Obliged," he said. "Not your man, however."

CHAPTER 6

Mallory's jaw sagged. He stared at Starbuck in amazed disbelief. "What?"

"Said I wasn't interested."

The rancher heaved his large bulk upright, face flushed with anger. "You know what you're doing? You're turning down the job of being top hand on the best goddam cattle ranch in the country — you realize that?"

Shawn nodded.

"Hell, I'm offering you the chance of your life."

Starbuck remained silent. Mallory brushed irritably at the fresh flow of sweat breaking out on his forehead. "Then what the devil is it? Working for Stingaree's something a lot of men would give their right arm to do. Means plenty in this country. Stingaree hands are looked up to — reckon you could say folks even fear them. Nobody ever tries anything with one of my boys. Know damn well the whole push'll be down on them if they do.

"One of the reasons I named my ranch Stingaree, for one of them water scorpions you find out along the ocean. Man messes with one of them, steps on it or grabs a hold, he gets hurt right quick. Way it is here — and everybody knows it. Worth plenty to be riding for an outfit like mine."

Starbuck, motionless in the shadowy office, arms folded, legs spread, smiled faintly as the rancher rushed on.

"You want more money? I'm willing if you step in, take hold, and prove you're worth it. Never held back yet on paying a man what he earned. Got a reputation for that. Nobody pays regular cowpunchers good as I do!"

"Not the money —"

"Then what —"

"I'll have no part in driving a man, any man, off his land," Shawn said bluntly.

"Not exactly the way of it. I'm paying hard cash for what they've got."

"No difference — and it's at your price. You ride a man into the ground, get him where he can't move, then toss him a few dollars and take over his place."

"What's wrong with that?" Mallory demanded. "In this country it's the hard, tough ones that win out and keep living. No place here for the dudes and the milk-sops and the weak-kneed psalm singers!"

"They probably could make a go of it if

you and your kind would leave them alone. Expect most of the people you've driven off their land didn't give up because they were weak but because they didn't have the money to hire on gunslingers for protection."

"That's why they were weak! Money makes for strength, and them that don't have it can't stand up to them that do. That's what makes the difference — and that's the way it's supposed to be."

"Doubt that."

"You doubt it — what the hell does a saddlebum like you know about it? In this life it's the strong ones that have to take over. Was it left up to the sodbusters and shirttail ranchers this country'd go to hell in a basket mighty quick! What happens when a bad year comes along — a winter freeze, or a drought, or maybe a grass fire that the wind spreads over the whole damned place?

"They're wiped out, that's what. They don't have anything to fall back on, and they're done for. Stingaree can stand up against the worst of all of it. My boys keep right on working and drawing their wages — and the Territory keeps on collecting its taxes. And far as the eastern cattle markets are concerned, business goes right on.

"If it wasn't for an outfit like mine,

everybody'd get hurt when times are hard. Way it is the wheels keep turning and it's good for everybody instead of being bad. You've got to admit that's right."

"For you, maybe," Starbuck said quietly, "but not for the man with a small outfit trying to make a go of it. He figures on hard times, looks at it as part of the price he has to pay — something he's ready and willing to do. If he wasn't, the small ranchers and the homesteaders would've died out long ago."

Mallory spat, brushed at his lips. "You trying to tell me them little hard-rock outfits like being poor?"

"No, not saying that. Said they expect it, figure on it. All a part of living, and when something wipes them out, they're proud to get up and start over again. It's in the way they're made."

Mallory snorted in disgust. "That's a crock of bull! Me or nobody else'll ever swallow that. I know their kind — worthless, shiftless, living from hand to mouth —"

"Some, not most."

"Sure covers the ones I've run up against, and they were all a hell of a lot better off after I got done with them. Goes for Handleman and Lockridge and all the others, too."

"Rafferty?"

"Him, same as the rest."

"Can't put him in the same bucket as the ones you've been talking about. He's got a big place, doing fine, I hear, and not in need of your money."

King Mallory's face darkened. "Different matter. I need that land. Blocks me off from the north part of the valley. Same as cuts Stingaree in two."

"Plenty of room to go around."

"Not about to bother doing that. Rafferty's finished, anyway. He don't need to ranch. Got all the money he'll ever spend and he's letting the place go to ruin. Instead of growing, he's standing still, or maybe even sliding downhill."

"Could be he figures he's got it made, now wants to just sit back and take it easy, enjoy what he's built."

"Not it at all! Bullheaded, that's what he is. Knows I need his place so he's bowed his neck and won't sell. . . . But he will though, by God! He'll come to it!"

"I don't know Rafferty but he might surprise you."

"Not him —"

"You're not dealing with a small outfit when you take him on. Expect he's got the cash and the men, and there'll likely be a lot of people stand by him. Would myself."

The rancher started to speak, hesitated, eyes drilling into Shawn. "You'd work — fight — for him but not for me?"

Starbuck nodded.

"Why? Why would you side Rafferty and not me?"

"Because he's in the right and you're not. He'll be fighting for what's his. You're trying to take it away from him."

Mallory swore deeply, wagged his head. "What the hell are you, some kind of a do-gooder? I figured you for a genuine stem-winder of a man who knowed what's what. Turns out you ain't nothing but show."

Starbuck's temper was finally beginning to get the best of him. He'd listened patiently to the rancher's ramblings, held his tongue as much as possible in deference to the politeness bred into him, but now Mallory, unable to have his way, was turning ugly.

"I'll let that pass," Shawn murmured.

"Kind of expected you would," the rancher said scornfully, coming from behind his desk and circling around to the front. "Seems I made a hell of a mistake about you, and when I make a mistake, I fix it quick. Now, draw your time and move on. Come morning, I don't want to see you on my land. No place on Stingaree for a man

59

with a yellow streak wide as yours."

Disgust, anger, and disapproval, combining into a hot, swelling flood within Starbuck, brimmed abruptly. He wheeled swiftly, drove his fist wrist-deep into King Mallory's overhanging belly.

"I'll be gone," he said curtly to the gasping, spread-eyed man. "Nothing could keep me here."

CHAPTER 7

Grim, Starbuck stepped through the doorway, paused on the stoop. Caleb and Emmett Stark were waiting on the bunkhouse porch for him, either to go for the evening meal together or out of curiosity as to Mallory's calling him. Over to the left Frank Price stood in front of his quarters, his shadowed features stiff as he waited apprehensively for some indication of the meeting's purpose.

Moving off the square of boards, Shawn angled across the hardpack for the foreman. In the half dark he saw Price draw up and he felt a stir of pity for him.

"Been ordered off the place," he said immediately as he halted before the man. "Like to draw what wages I've got coming."

Relief flooded Price's face. His shoulders relaxed gently. "Right now?"

"Morning'll do," Starbuck said and cut back toward the bunkhouse.

Caleb greeted him with a slow smile. "Well, you the new ramrod of this here outfit?"

"Hardly," Shawn replied shortly. The

anger aroused by King Mallory had not yet fully dissipated and there was a sharpness to his manner. "Fact is, I don't work here any more."

"You quit?" Stark asked, surprised.

"Fired."

Fain spat. "Hell, King sure didn't call you in to tell you he was firing you. Something else happened — and what was you telling Frank?"

Starbuck grinned in spite of himself at the old wrangler's bald curiosity. "That I'd be leaving and wanted to draw my time."

"Reckon that was good news to him. He was worried plumb sick figuring King called you in to give you his job."

"Just don't savvy," Emmett said, scratching at his jaw. "Was only a couple, three hours ago you was telling me how you liked this job, then you up and quit. Why?"

"Wanted me to take McCoskey's job. I'm not interested in that sort of work. . . . What do you say we eat?"

Caleb and Stark were staring at Shawn. The younger man swore, said, "McCoskey's job — means you'd be heading up the bully-boys."

"Starting tonight."

"They doing some raiding tonight?" Caleb asked quickly. "Rafferty, I expect."

Shawn shrugged faintly, neither confirming nor denying, and turned toward the cook shack. Silent, the two men fell in beside him.

Most of the off-duty crew were there, including Rafe McCoskey and those that ran with him — except for Jack Mallory, who still took his meals at the house with the rest of his family.

Starbuck, Fain, and Emmett Stark found places at the long table, began to fill their plates. The young Mexican boy who served as cook's helper came up, served them coffee from a steaming, granite pot, and moved on down the line to replenish the cups of others ready for seconds or thirds.

The meal was eaten in near silence, only the clatter of knives and forks, an occasional grunt of satisfaction, or a request for some item beyond reach breaking the hush. When it was about finished, Stark leaned toward Shawn.

"You reckon I'd be smart to hit Mallory up for that job?"

Starbuck considered the question for several moments. "Could be," he said finally, "if you've got a feeling for that kind of work."

"How am I to know? Never tried it."

Shawn ducked his head at McCoskey sit-

63

ting across the table and down a few places with his followers. "Take a look at him. If you figure you can be like him, then go talk to Mallory."

Emmett studied the gunman for a time, shook his head. "Let's me out, I reckon. Was I like that I purely couldn't stand myself."

"Where you heading when you leave?" Fain asked, hooking a finger in his tin cup's handle and leaning back.

"South. Got to scrape up another job. Quite a few ranches down that way, I remember."

"This time of year jobs ain't so plentiful."

"Know that, and I'm not particular except when it comes to doing some things."

"Expect King offered you plenty to run them Troubleshooters for him."

Starbuck nodded. "He was willing to pay plenty, but sometimes the money you get for a job's not worth what you have to do to earn it."

"For sure," Caleb agreed. "Recollect one I had up Cheyenne way before I tied up with Mallory. Was skinning mules for a freight outfit. Was the miserablest job I ever had. Road agents always laying for me, Injuns popping out of the brush ever whichaway —

and the wind! It blowed all the time, and so danged hard that was a man to shoot into it, the bullets come right back at him!"

The wrangler paused, smiling wryly at the recollection. Then, taking a swallow of his coffee, he turned again to Shawn.

"Mind me asking you something? Been bothering me ever since you showed up here, and now with you a-leaving, it's itching me something fierce."

"Go ahead."

"That there belt buckle you're wearing with one of them fancy boxer fellows on it. Sure is a mighty handsome piece of foofaraw. It mean something special, like maybe you was once a champion?"

Starbuck took the oblong of scrolled silver with its superimposed ivory figure between a thumb and forefinger and tipped it upward so that the two men might have a better look.

"Been wondering about it myself," Stark said. "After I seen you clean Tom Dillard's plow out there on the range, I figured it was something more than for just holding up your pants."

"Belonged to my pa," Shawn explained. "He was good at boxing — scientific fighting, they call it. He used to put on exhibition matches about every weekend back home. Learned how from some friend of his that came over here from England."

"It was your pa then that was the champion —"

"No. Expect he could've been had he wanted to keep at it. Was a farmer, though, and that's what he liked best."

"Remembering how you licked old Tom to a frazzle, I'd say he taught you plenty."

"Both me and my brother, Ben. We had regular lessons."

"You ever put on one of them exhibitions?"

"No, only use what I know about it when I have to. Seems Ben does. I've heard of a few matches he's held. Expect he's about as good as Pa by now."

"With that sort've being his calling, I wouldn't think it'd be hard to run him down," Stark said. "Sure ain't many men fighting that way in this part of the country."

"About right. Only thing is my luck's always been bad — late, you might say. Hear about a match after it's all over with. Closest I came was up in New Mexico. Town called Silver City. I got there the day after it was all over with."

"Well, I sure hope you find him one of these days," Caleb said. "Be a shame was you to spend your life chasing after him — and never catching up. It's real important —"

The old man broke off as King Mallory, looking no worse for wear, appeared in the doorway. Caleb rocked forward, and lowering his voice said, "Here's the old he-goat hisself — and looking about as happy as a man who's just had to shoot his best horse."

Noise and what little conversation was underway died off as the rancher stepped into the room and glanced around. His hard eyes settled upon Starbuck, brought a quick tightening of his mouth. Circling the end of the table, huge bulk setting the floor to squeaking as he walked, he strode to where Shawn sat.

"Told you to get the hell off my ranch!"

"Aim to, in the morning," Starbuck replied evenly.

"You're getting off now — tonight!" Mallory shouted, and dug into a pocket. Procuring a handful of coins, he selected two double eagles, tossed them into Shawn's plate.

"That's more'n you've got coming. Take it and ride. I see you around here agin, I'll use my gun!" Abruptly he turned away, threw his glance farther down the table. "McCoskey!"

"Right here, Mr. Mallory."

"We're riding tonight. Want you and your bunch ready to go in one hour."

The gunman nodded indifferently. "Yessir, Mr. Mallory," he drawled.

The rancher's eyes glowed with greater anger at the rankling tone of the man, but he said no more. Pivoting on a heel, he retraced his steps to the doorway and disappeared into the darkness.

"Whoo — ee!" Caleb Fain murmured. "He sure is steamed up something fierce. You sure all you done to him was quit?"

Starbuck shrugged, picked up the two gold pieces. Brushing off the food crumbs, he slipped them into his shirt pocket, aware of the curious glances being cast his way. Rafe McCoskey rattled his tin cup for more coffee, settled his small, dark eyes on Shawn.

"You and the old stud have some words?"

Starbuck nodded. He wanted no problems with the gunman. "A few."

Rafe grinned knowingly. "Always figured you was a mite too big for your britches. What was it all about?"

"Ask him."

"Asking you. It'll be me that'll have to use a gun on you, not him, does it have to be, and I always like to know why I'm shooting a man."

68

Temper was rising once again in Starbuck. "Let it drop, Rafe," he said softly.

The smirk faded gradually on McCoskey's face as he continued to study Shawn. Finally, he turned to his now re-filled coffee cup. Glancing about, he grinned broadly.

"Ought to have some red-eye for this," he said in a loud voice. "Going to have a right busy night. Need something stronger'n this to hot up my innards."

"Got a bottle in my saddlebags," the rider next to him volunteered.

"Now, that's mighty fine, Ed. You just trot over and get it. Want all you boys to stoke your bellies good."

Starbuck pushed back from the table and got to his feet. Stark and Caleb followed quickly. Conscious of the wondering atten-tion still being accorded him, he looked over his shoulder, nodded briefly, and moved on toward the doorway.

CHAPTER 8

"You pulling out tonight, like King said?" Caleb asked as they stepped down into the yard.

"What he wants," Starbuck replied, turning toward the corrals.

"Hell, could stay 'til morning. He'd never know the difference."

"Maybe not," Shawn said, glancing at the long, rambling ranchhouse. Lamplight glowed in several windows, and two horses, saddled and ready for use, stood at the hitchrack.

"You wouldn't be worrying about that talking Rafe McCoskey was doing, would you?"

Shawn halted at the corral. "Hardly," he said with a half smile, and opening the gate, he entered the enclosure. Singling out the sorrel, he threw on his gear and then led the big gelding back into the yard. As they started for the bunkhouse Emmett Stark spoke.

"You could put yourself up in that old line shack on the south range. Ain't never used no more."

"Room in town will do fine," Starbuck said, determined to comply with the rancher's wishes. He'd had his fill of the man and ignoring his demands would only lead to unnecessary trouble.

They reached the crew's quarters. Shawn left the sorrel at the rack, and with Stark and Caleb trailing him, crossed the porch and entered. A card game was in progress on a blanket spread on the floor. A half dozen players were gathered around it. As Shawn moved by, pointing for his bunk to collect his personal belongings, all looked up.

"Sure hate seeing you leave," one said.

"No more than I hate going," Starbuck answered. "Was a good job."

"You sure must've put a burr under the old man's blanket. What'd you do to rile him up so?"

"Said no to him," Shawn replied, laconically.

Caleb Fain laughed. "And that's sure something a fellow hadn't ought to do. He ain't used to being —"

"No to what?" Ramsey, a squat Texan, also one of the poker players, asked.

Starbuck halted at his bunk. Laying out his saddlebags, he began to stow his belongings into its deep pockets.

"Just a little proposition he had in mind,"

71

he said in a tone that indicated the subject was closed.

Stark stretched out on the bunk opposite, watched Shawn quietly. Caleb Fain drifted away after a few moments, fell to watching the card game, adding with his charred pipe to the cigarette smoke hanging from the ceiling in a thin, blue cloud.

"You figure to lay around town a spell?" Emmett asked, finally breaking his silence.

"Maybe, and I might just ride on in the morning. No reason to stay."

The puncher sighed heavily. "Kind of wish I was going along. If it wasn't for — well, you know who —"

Starbuck nodded, buckling the straps of his leather pouches. Always on the move, he had taken pains not to accumulate much, only the necessities such as a change of clothing, shaving equipment, the implements needed for cooking and the like.

"Reckon that does it," he announced, straightening up, and glanced toward the doorway.

Rafe McCoskey, accompanied by several of the men who rode with him, entered the haze-filled room. The gunman's features were flushed, his eyes unnaturally bright. It was evident he had partaken liberally of the whiskey his friend had provided.

Grinning broadly, he swaggered past the card players, kneeing one roughly in the back, and halted in front of Shawn.

"Why the hell ain't you gone?" he demanded, letting the grin die. "Heard King tell you to get."

It was Starbuck's turn to smile. No one dared call the rancher by his first name and McCoskey was doing so only because Mallory was not within hearing distance.

"He's just leaving," Stark said, sitting up.

"Well, he ain't doing it fast enough," McCoskey snapped, centering his gaze on Shawn again. "King told you to ride. I'm here to see you do it."

Caleb Fain pushed forward. "What the hell, Rafe! He ain't had time to —"

Starbuck silenced the old wrangler with a raised hand. He'd never had any problems with the gunman, probably because, as a group, they kept themselves apart from the working crew. It would seem now, however, that McCoskey had come looking for trouble — and Shawn was in no mood to sidestep it. "He send you to find out?"

"Didn't need to. King wants a job done — I do it."

The room was in utter silence. Fain moved up to where he stood beside Emmett Stark.

73

"I'll bet you're a real big help to him," Starbuck said, slinging his saddlebags over a shoulder. "Now, get out of my way."

McCoskey's shoulders came back slowly. His jaw tightened as his hands dropped to his sides. "Ain't nobody talks to me like that."

Shawn allowed the saddlebags to slide away, caught them with his hand, and laid them back on the bunk. The gunman was motionless, flushed face devoid of all expression as he watched.

Starbuck turned lazily to him. "Any time," he said coolly.

Outside the thud of horses' hooves on the hardpack sounded. A moment later King Mallory's impatient voice called.

"Rafe — you in there?"

Immediately the brittle tension broke. McCoskey's rigid shape relented. Shrugging, he pivoted to the door.

"Yessir, Mr. Mallory. We're all ready."

"Then get out here and let's get going!"

The gunman paused at the opening, flung a glance back to Starbuck. "We ain't done yet — you and me."

Shawn took up his saddlebags once more. "Sure, sure," he said quietly.

Emmett Stark, alone in the darkness of

74

the yard, leaned against the corral fence and watched Starbuck ride off into the night. He hated to see the man leave. Shawn had been the nearest thing to a best friend he'd ever had, and being a person with an easy-going nature, he'd made quite a few acquaintances in his lifetime.

Starbuck was different from the others, however. Big, strong, quietly expert, he seemed able to handle anything, meet any crisis. Like calling McCoskey's bluff. Never before had anyone dared to cross Rafe, but Shawn had stopped him cold. It was a good thing for him that King Mallory had showed up when he did, otherwise they'd either be burying the gunman, or digging a bullet out of him. But it was doubtful McCoskey would have let it go that far. You could see in his eyes that he suddenly wanted no part of Starbuck.

He wished again he had been free to go with the big drifter, but with matters standing the way they did between him and Chris, he just couldn't do it. She needed him, really and truly did, what with her pa and brother being the way they were. Dammit! Why couldn't he figure out how he could be of some use to her? Starbuck would.

He wondered again about the job —

McCoskey's job, that Shawn had turned down, speculated on the possibility of asking Mallory for a crack at it. His ability fell far short of Starbuck's, he knew, but by God, he was just as good a man as Rafe McCoskey! Rafe could use a gun but that's where it ended — and if he'd do a little practicing himself, he could make up that difference.

It sure would be a lot easier for him and Chris if her pa would give him his chance and he showed up good. At least, he thought it would. It was hard to be sure. A man never knew just how Mallory would react — and he was strict as hell about Chris having anything to do with the hired help. Might be worth the try, though. If he could talk himself into a better job with the rancher and then later let it be known that he was interested in Chris, things just might come out fine. If they didn't, well, he and Chris would just have to keep on the way they were, meeting on the sly and such — assuming Mallory didn't blow up and run him off.

Too, after this night matters could be better at Stingaree. Mallory had ridden out with McCoskey and his bunch of hardcases to pay a call on Rafferty, and it was well known that Arrowhead was the last big ranch in the Gila that King was out to get. If it worked out the way he wanted it to, the rancher would have little use from then on for the talents of Rafe and his crowd. Most anybody would be able to wind up the rest of the business that Mallory had in mind.

"Me, for instance," Stark muttered aloud. Maybe he'd never be the stem-winder McCoskey was with a six-gun, but no expert would be needed to handle the two homesteaders and that rancher north of Arrowhead.

By God, he'd hit Mallory up for the job when he got back, or leastwise, he would in the morning. Mallory couldn't do no more than say no. He wished now he'd been thinking straight and volunteered to go along on the raid. Maybe something would have happened to make Mallory notice him and sort of put him in good. But that's the way it had always been for him — a day late or a dollar short.

Stark drew up slowly. Could be he wasn't too late! Why not saddle up and try catching them? They'd only been gone a few minutes, and riding fast, and with a bit of luck, he'd probably overtake the party.

Wheeling, Emmett Stark trotted hurriedly to the corral where he'd slung his gear and left his horse. All he wanted was a chance to show King Mallory he had what it takes to do a job; like as not he'd find the opportunity that night at Arrowhead.

CHAPTER 9

Starbuck roused at the first insistent rap on the door. He lay there quietly, frowning, wondering who it might be at that hour of the night.

Earlier, after a drink at the bar, he had checked into the room, one of the small, rear, poorly furnished cubicles on the upper floor of Kottman's Saloon, and retired. Subsequently, three knocks had sounded; one, a drunk searching for a friend, the others, female inquirers asking if he desired companionship. Finally he'd gotten to sleep — but now this.

"Who is it?" he called impatiently.

"Me — Caleb. Got to see you."

Shawn threw his legs over the edge of the bed, rose and crossed to the door, wondering as he did about the purpose of the older man's. . . . If he'd come into town, gotten himself all liquored up . . . Turning the key in the lock, he jerked open the flimsy panel.

"What —" he began, and stopped.

Fain was far from being drunk. His seamy face was sober and strain showed in his eyes.

He stepped quickly into the room, pulled off his hat.

"Mallory's dead," he said grimly.

Starbuck pushed the door closed, returned to the bed and sat down. "Too bad, but it's something I reckon everybody expected. He couldn't keep running roughshod over folks and get away with it forever. It happen at Rafferty's?"

Caleb shook his head. "Ain't sure."

Shawn glanced up in surprise. "He was going there with McCoskey and his bunch. Planned to tear up the place some. There would've been shooting."

"He done that, sure enough. Rafe said he seen him once while things was popping, then when it was all over King wasn't around."

"Then what —"

"Stark hauled him in across his saddle. Claims he rode out to do some talking to Mallory, found him laying dead alongside the trail."

Starbuck rolled Fain's words about in his mind. "You saying that maybe Emmett killed him?"

"Nope, I sure ain't, but McCoskey's sort of spreading the idea around. Way he tells it King never mixes in much when the fireworks are going on, just sort of sets back,

80

watches so there ain't much chance of him catching a bullet. . . . You think Emmett could've done it? Had himself a real good reason, I expect."

Starbuck looked more closely at the older man. "What's that?"

Caleb shrugged, leaned against the wall. Brushing at the sweat on his face, he said, "Hell, you think I don't know about him and King's gal? Come across them two or three times but I didn't let them see me. There'd a been the devil to pay if King'd heard about it, but with him out of the way —"

"They had a problem, all right, and Emmett was plenty jumpy about Mallory, but he'd never kill him. I'd lay odds on that. Can think of a couple others who'd be better prospects."

"Who'd that be?"

"Jack Mallory for one. Easy to see he hated his pa — and with him dead he'll be in line to take over the ranch, run it to suit himself. And there's McCoskey. He might be King Mallory's right hand and chief gun-slinger but he hated his guts because of the way Mallory treated him. Anybody could see that."

Caleb nodded. "Sure can't fault you there."

"Take those two and add the names of the

people he's robbed of their land and you'll have yourself a pretty fair list."

"For a fact, and I reckon you could figure the gal in on it, too. She sure didn't have no use for her pa, either. He was always queering things for her — with the boys she took a fancy to, I mean."

"Maybe, but whether he got shot during the raid or somebody bushwhacked him is for the law to find out and no business of mine —"

"Hell, I plumb near forgot what I come for!" Fain broke in. "Got so wound up talking it plain slipped my mind."

"What did?" Starbuck asked, yawning.

"Reason I'm here. Missus Mallory wants to see you."

"Me?" Shawn exclaimed in surprise. "I don't know her and she sure doesn't know me. Only seen her a couple of times and that was at a distance."

"Maybe so, but she's wanting to talk to you."

"She send you?"

"No, was Stark. She told him, I reckon. He sent me to fetch you."

Shawn did not stir. He cared little about King Mallory and what had happened to him. The rancher, cold-blooded, ruthless, and utterly selfish, had earned what he'd finally received, and while justice should be served if there was murder involved, it was a job better handled by someone else less acquainted with Mallory.

Too, he was reluctant to become mixed up in a situation that would delay and hinder him in the search for Ben. All too often he'd gotten himself bogged down in other folks' problems, sometimes to the extent of actually missing out on an opportunity that would have brought him and his brother together.

Besides, what could King Mallory's widow want of him? He knew nothing of what had transpired. His altercation with the rancher had taken place long before he'd ridden out with his Troubleshooters to raid Rafferty's Arrowhead.

"You coming?" Caleb asked.

Starbuck shook his head. "Don't see how I can help."

"She figures you can — seems."

"Best thing for her to do is call in the law, let them handle it."

"Ain't no law around close. . . . I ain't sure just what's going on, but I sort've got the idea from Emmett that she's plenty worried and needing help bad."

Starbuck considered that in silence. It wasn't in him to turn his back on anyone in trouble, but in this instance he failed to see what use he could be.

"Makes no sense," he said. "She's got plenty of good help — you, Emmett, Frank Price —"

"And she's got Jack and Rafe McCoskey, too. I'm thinking that's what's bothering her."

Shawn nodded slowly. It would be McCoskey, of course. In him she saw a serious threat. Rising, he turned to the scarred rocking chair beside the bed on which he'd draped his clothing and began to dress.

"Be ready in a couple of minutes," he said.

CHAPTER 10

It was still an hour or two before daylight when Shawn and Caleb Fain rode into Stingaree. The windows of the main house as well as the crew's quarters were ablaze with light and even the cook was up, had coffee ready for those who wanted it.

He saw McCoskey at once. The gunman and four of his men were standing near the gate a hundred yards or so beyond the house as if on sentry duty. Caleb noted his attention.

"Keeping their eyes peeled for the Arrowhead bunch. Everybody's looking for Rafferty to hit back."

"Probably will," Starbuck said, drawing the sorrel to a halt at the hitchrack.

"Ain't no probably to it! Hell's done opened the gates now. This here Gila Valley's going to be like a second Gettysburg when the word leaks out that King's dead."

Shawn had to agree. Not only could Stingaree look for retaliation from Boone Rafferty, but all of the other ranchers and homesteaders who'd felt the crunch of Mallory's heel would rally to strike back at their common enemy. The fact that King Mallory was dead and therefore unknowing would not matter; Stingaree was still there, and Stingaree and those who were a part of it would become the whipping boy.

Dismounting, Starbuck looped the leathers around the rack's crossbar, paused as Caleb's low, warning voice reached him.

"Watch yourself. Here comes Rafe."

Shawn wheeled slowly. McCoskey, features set, a rifle in his hands, approached angrily.

"What're you doing back here? King told you to clear out."

"I brung him," Caleb said before Starbuck could answer.

"You! Who the hell give you —"

"Was Missus Mallory sent for him. You want to do some argufying, go see her."

McCoskey frowned. In the pale glow of the bunkhouse lamps shining through the windows, his face looked deep-lined and swarthy.

"I didn't hear Jack say nothing about him."

"Reckon that's because Jack ain't running things," Fain said coolly, and taking Starbuck by the elbow, he started toward the main house. "Let's be getting up there."

Instantly the gunman reached out, caught

Shawn's opposite arm. "You ain't going nowheres 'til I talk to Jack!"

Starbuck, in no pleasant mood at best, spun swiftly. His hand came up, knocked the rifle from McCoskey's grasp, sent it spinning to the ground. The gunman yelled, jumped back, fingers wrapping about the butt of the pistol on his hip. He froze, seeing the round muzzle of Starbuck's weapon leveled at him.

"You've been wanting this," Shawn murmured. "Now's the time to get it over with."

Rafe McCoskey did not stir for a long minute, and then he shrugged. "I'll pick the time," he said and turned away.

Starbuck, not trusting the man at all, watched him move off, striking for the gate where his friends waited.

"You're a fool if you let him do the choosing," Caleb muttered, his eyes also on the gunman. "Time he'll pick'll be some dark night when you're looking the other way."

"He's the kind," Shawn replied.

He was not thinking so much of that, however, as he was of what McCoskey had said about Jack Mallory. It was evident the son was intending to take over Stingaree, while, judging from Caleb's words, the rancher's widow was assuming command. If

87

such proved to be true there was plenty of trouble ahead for Stingaree — not only from outsiders but from Mallory's men as well. The place would split wide open, with some of the crew, including McCoskey and the Troubleshooters, lining up with Jack, the rest siding Mrs. Mallory — and with him caught somewhere in the middle.

Shawn sighed heavily. He could do without all of it, just as Stingaree could get by without any internal strife, considering Arrowhead and all the others who'd be getting in their licks. They'd best heed the words he'd once read in a schoolbook: *hang together or likely they'll hang separately.*

But there was no denying that the younger Mallory had a claim. He gave that thought as he and Caleb moved on toward the house, soon turned to him.

"Times like this the son usually takes over. You think if Jack straightened out, shed himself of McCoskey and his bunch, he could run this ranch?"

Fain snorted. "Not much, he could. Only running he'd do would be straight into the ground."

"This could change him, turn him into a man."

"Maybe it would've if King had brung him up different. Never give him a chance

88

to learn nothing of the right kind — like now. Jack wouldn't know what to do, and he'd be listening all the time to Rafe — he wouldn't get rid of him like you said. Rafe'd be the kingpin around here, and you know what that'd mean."

"Mean the end of Stingaree," Shawn admitted, "figuring it survives Arrowhead and all the rest that'll be kicking at the gates."

"Amen," Caleb said.

"Be a shame. Didn't like Mallory and his way of doing things, but he built a fine ranch. Shouldn't be let go to hell."

"Way I feel about it, too. Was some truth in the things King was always saying about it being good for the country and such."

Far back on the slopes beyond the ranch a wolf howled into the graying night. It was an eerie, wailing sound that seemed to echo endlessly. Caleb swore softly.

"Sure is a creepy thing. Sort of puts the chills in a man — like maybe that old lobo was mourning for King."

Two of a kind, Starbuck thought but he did not voice the words. Speaking ill of King Mallory would accomplish nothing. What the man had done, was done, and neither praise nor rebuke would change any of it.

He glanced up. The ranchhouse, strong, solidly built, its windows alight, was before him. Again he wondered at the real reason for being summoned. Evidently Mrs. Mallory believed he knew something that would be of value to her.

Was it possible the rancher had mentioned his name to her, telling her of his intentions to offer him a better job? Perhaps she was going to repeat the proposition. He mulled that over, tried to decide then, beforehand, if he'd be interested. The answer was no if she planned to carry on in the boot-tracks of her husband. She had Jack and Rafe McCoskey for that. If it was something else —

"You right sure you don't know what Mrs. Mallory wants with me?" he asked again of Fain.

"Ain't got the littlest hunch," Caleb replied. "All I know is Emmett said to fetch you, make you come back no matter what."

"It's bothering me some. Don't like walking in there without knowing what I'm getting into. Was thinking she might be wanting me to take the job Mallory offered."

"Rafe's job?"

Shawn nodded.

"Nope, don't figure that's it. She's got Rafe and Jack, was she aiming to be like King."

"Probably going to need them," Starbuck

said. "Not to do any raiding but to fight them off. How long do you think it'll take before word of Mallory's death gets out?"

"About one day — and that's guessing it close. News like that travels mighty fast."

"You mention it to anybody around Kottman's when you came after me?"

"Nope. Weren't nobody awake 'cepting some drifters nursing a bottle in the corner of the saloon. Even the gal setting with them had dozed off."

"That'll give the Mallorys a bit of leeway. Can use it to bury King."

"Be doing that here. He rigged up two graveyards out on the hill south of the house. Heard him tell his folks had their own burying place back in Tennessee, wanted to do the same here. . . . Kind of funny, it being him that's going to be the first one planted in it."

"You said two graveyards —"

"Other'ns for the hired help. There's quite a few in it. Was a dozen or more that got themselves killed helping him build this here ranch. Maybe a couple or three that died, natural-like."

Caleb paused at the foot of the steps leading up onto the porch. "Here we be. Reckon I'd best wait out here. She didn't send for me."

"You can probably do her more good than I can," Starbuck said, aware of the faint bitterness in the older man's tone. He dropped a hand on Fain's shoulder. "Ought to be right out. I don't figure this will take long."

CHAPTER 11

Emmett Stark, face long and solemn, met him at the door.

"Obliged to you for coming back," he said, and nodding toward a room to their left, added, "They're in there, the parlor, waiting."

Starbuck, unmoving, said, "Who's waiting?"

"Mrs. Mallory and Chris. And Jack."

"What do they want from me?"

"Mrs. Mallory wants to talk to you about the ranch."

Reluctant, Shawn shook his head. "She doesn't know me from Adam. Why'd she pick me?"

"Probably because I told her about you," Stark said. "Come on."

Shrugging, Starbuck removed his hat and followed the puncher across the entry way into a large room well filled with heavy furniture, thick carpets, and gilt-framed portraits. A half dozen lamps burned on as many tables. One thing he guessed he could say about King Mallory was that he hadn't stinted insofar as his home was concerned.

Two women, Christine and the rancher's widow, were seated on a brocaded divan placed against an inside wall. Jack, not entirely sober, stood nearby. Stark halted before them.

"This here's the man I was telling you about, Mrs. Mallory. Name's Shawn Starbuck."

The woman smiled faintly. She was slender, had blue eyes and chestnut hair now showing streaks of gray. That Christine was a duplicate of her in appearance was evident.

"I'm Theodosia Mallory, Mr. Starbuck," she said quietly.

"My pleasure, ma'am," Shawn said, accepting the hand she offered.

Her clasp was firm and steady, and she had a direct way of meeting his gaze that at once altered the opinion he'd formed of her. She might have been overshadowed, even dominated by King Mallory, but there it had undoubtedly ended.

"Emmett has told me a lot about you," she said in a low, controlled voice. "I appreciate your coming here at this hour, and apologize, but because of my husband's death, I felt it was necessary."

There was little grief or sadness in the

room, Starbuck realized, and supposed he could understand why. Still, King Mallory had been the husband and father, had given them much, and despite all else, in death he was entitled to some consideration.

"I believe we should take matters in hand as quickly as possible," the woman finished.

She was a smart one, all right. She knew there would be repercussions from Boone Rafferty as well as others, and she didn't want to be caught napping.

"I figure we can run things without no outside help," Jack said impatiently. "Fact is, I've got Rafe and the boys all set right now. If anybody tries —"

"Which is just what I want to avoid — trouble and bloodshed," Mrs. Mallory said firmly.

"Too late for that," Mallory snapped. "And if we're going to keep this place going right we'll have to be tough, just like Pa, and keep on being tough."

Theodosia Mallory folded her hands in her lap, studied them thoughtfully. "What do you say to that, Mr. Starbuck?"

"No doubt you're in for trouble. Plenty of folks around who don't like your husband, and they won't be forgetting just because he's gone. I figure there's two ways to handle it — talk to them, do whatever it takes to satisfy them, or follow Jack's plan."

"I'd be doing like Pa would —"

"Your father's dead, Jack. I'll decide now what's best for us."

"You!" Mallory blurted angrily. "Supposed to be me taking over. I'm the son —"

"I only wish you could," the woman said wearily.

"Well, you trying to do things your way — patting everybody with a gripe on the head, telling them you're sorry, giving in to them, sure ain't the way to run Stingaree! Place'll go to hell mighty fast, you try that!"

"Jack!" Christine exclaimed. "Don't you talk like that to Mother!"

"Aim to talk any way I please!" Mallory shot back. "I'm the head of this house now, and everybody's going to listen to me!"

"I shan't! Mother's going to —"

"You shut up!" Jack raged. "You've got nothing to say, and if you want to marry that cowhand you're so sweet on, then do it and get out! Now, I'm starting right in doing what I ought. First, I want Starbuck gone. You hadn't ought've called him back — not after Pa ran him off."

Theodosia Mallory, calm despite the outburst, turned her attention to Shawn. "Do you mind telling me why?"

"He offered me the kind of a job I won't

96

take," Starbuck replied. "We had a few words over it."

"Job — what job?" Jack demanded.

"McCoskey's."

"That's a lie! Pa wouldn't junk Rafe for you!"

Starbuck's temper lifted, leveled off as he considered the source and circumstances. "Was what it was about. Whether you believe it or not means nothing to me."

Emmett Stark moved to where he stood beside Christine. "You can believe it," he said, nodding to Mrs. Mallory. "When Shawn told me he'd turned it down, I had ideas myself of asking for it. Finally decided I would. Was why I rode out to find your husband. Aimed to talk to him, see if he'd give me a chance at it."

"You!" Jack laughed scornfully. "You take Rafe's job?"

"What I wanted — only I was too late to do any talking about it."

"Which seems mighty funny. Everybody else seen Pa alive. You're telling that he was already dead when you seen him. I'm thinking maybe it was you —"

Stark took a quick, angry step forward. Christine reached up, caught him by the arm. "Nonsense!" she said. "And I'm glad you didn't get Rafe McCoskey's job. I wouldn't want you to be like him."

"Your pa was dead when I found him," Stark said stubbornly. "You got to believe that."

"I do — and so does Mother."

"Well, me and a few others ain't so sure," Jack declared sullenly. "Aim to —"

"Never mind," Theodosia Mallory broke in quietly. She seemed strangely indifferent to the possibility that her husband died at the hands of a murderer. "We have no time for family quarrels."

"Family!" Jack shouted. "Since when's that cowhand family?"

"You have already mentioned it," the woman said coolly. "Christine and Emmett plan to marry. The ceremony will take place as soon as things settle down."

Ignoring her son's outraged glare, Mrs. Mallory turned her attention again to Shawn. "If you were in my position, faced with the problems I know will arise when word of my husband's death gets around, what would you do, Mr. Starbuck?"

"The name's Shawn. Being called mister always makes me uncomfortable."

"All right, Shawn."

Starbuck shook his head. "Don't know where you got the idea that I'm something special at a time like this —"

98

"Emmett believes you are, and I trust his judgment."

"Could be he spread it on a little too thick, but since you've asked, I'll answer. Thing I'd do would be to try and stop the war before it got started."

"Won't be no war if we keep on doing the way Pa was!" Jack stated loudly. "Heard him tell Rafe once that it was fear that made Stingaree what it is, and that it'd take fear to keep it big and strong."

Theodosia sighed. "Fear is all this place has ever known — all it stands for. That's done with now. Your father's gone and I intend to change things."

"Then it'll be good-bye Stingaree!"

"No, I don't think so, Jack. I'm sure other ranches have become big and strong without fear, without guns and bloodshed. I don't see any reason why we can't do like them."

"Mostly because they won't ever let us, that's why. We ease off, back down and start treating people around here like we was running some kind of a Sunday sociable, they'll tear us to pieces."

"Do you think that's true, Shawn?"

Starbuck hesitated briefly, nodded. "Probably is," he said, and then as a puzzled frown crossed the woman's face, added, "I

99

agree that there ought to be a change. Stingaree should start dealing with other ranchers and homesteaders and such like they were human beings and have some rights, but at the same time you'll need to keep them thinking you're tough, too.

"Can do that without trampling on everybody. There's a big difference in being firm and being ruthless when you deal with a man."

Mrs. Mallory considered that quietly. Then, "I can see that Emmett was right," she said, and smiled up at Starbuck. "You don't look old enough to be so wise."

"Can't lay claim to that. Just happens I've knocked around the country quite a spell, and doing that, you sort've learn."

"Some can, others don't. What do you think I should do next?"

"Well, like I mentioned, get things headed off before they start. My guess is that after last night your biggest problem's going to be with Rafferty. Ought to get to him quick, try smoothing things over. You could offer to pay for all the damage that was done. Need to pacify him, keep him from raiding Stingaree the way your husband did his place last night.

"Then, the others that feel like they've got a call coming, the ones who lost their property to Stingaree, pass the word that you're willing to talk. Say you're willing to settle any grievance they've got, long as it's reasonable. You make the first move, do it before they start something and you'll take all the wind out of their sails."

Theodosia Mallory smiled, glanced to Christine and Emmett. "Those are the words I'd hope to hear — and the things I wanted to do only I didn't know how to begin."

"Figured Shawn would be coming up with the answer," Stark said, grinning.

The woman swung back to Starbuck. "I'm grateful to you, more than I can say."

"Glad to help —"

"I hope so, Shawn, because I'm going to ask a big favor of you. I want you to take the job of running Stingaree."

CHAPTER 12

So that was it. It wasn't advice or suggestions Theodosia Mallory sought, but help. She clearly believed her own son incapable, and Emmett Stark, while acceptable as a husband for her daughter, she evidently felt was not qualified to take over, either.

Did he want to become that deeply involved in what was not only going to become a family squabble but a tense, perhaps formidable situation with outsiders as well? He needed work, yes, had intended to start looking for a job that very day, but it was one of the ordinary sort he wanted — one that required only that he do an assigned task and placed neither authority nor serious responsibility on his shoulders.

It wasn't that he feared the pressures of such; it was simply that he was weary of being called upon to bear the worries of others. His place at Stingaree prior to the moments when he and King Mallory had come to a parting had been to his exact liking — good pay, decent food and quarters, ordinary, everyday cattle work. Too bad it had had to end.

Frowning, Starbuck stood there in the strong lamplight, a tall, muscled-out man seemingly well up in years but still young in actuality. In the glow his gray-blue eyes took on an almost colorless depth, and his dark hair, curling about his neck and ears in its need for trimming, appeared black.

"Don't know about that," he said, hesitantly.

"You're hunting a job," Emmett Stark pointed out quickly. "Said you aimed to start today. What's wrong with taking this one?"

Shawn stirred. "You're looking for a better one, right here on Stingaree. Why don't you take it?"

"Because I don't figure I'm big enough to handle it," Stark said frankly. "Did I, don't think I wouldn't jump at the chance."

"We discussed that earlier," Mrs. Mallory said. "I admire Emmett for his honesty — and that was when he told me about you. . . . Your wages, if you're wondering about them, will be up to you. I'm ready to pay any price if it will get things handled properly, once and for aii time."

"I'll tell you this!" Mallory warned. "I'm pulling out if you turn Stingaree over to him."

The woman faced her son, smiled sadly.

103

"I'm sorry, Jack. I only wish it could be you, but I daren't take the chance."

"A chance — on your own flesh and blood?"

"I'm afraid that's how it is. I'd hoped you'd not feel the way you do, but my mind is made up. I just don't want any more trouble — I want to be finished with it and guns and raids and people whispering behind my back about the Mallorys being thieves and pirates and such.

"You can't see it that way and Mr. Starbuck — Shawn — can. He thinks as I do, has the same intentions and knows how to make them come true. If you're forcing me to make a choice, it will have to be him."

Mallory, features flushed, eyes bright, wheeled to Starbuck. "Guess you're the key to what happens next. What's your answer?"

Starbuck glanced at the faces turned to him, read the quiet appeal in Theodosia Mallory's eyes, the hope in those of her daughter and of Emmett Stark — the resentment burning fiercely in Jack's. Again he felt strong reluctance. It would be no easy, simple task, and that he could expect trouble from Jack, assisted no doubt by Rafe McCoskey, was a certainty.

Nor could he be too positive of continual

support from Mrs. Mallory. She was making a choice now, but Jack was her own son, and as time wore on and the crisis tapered, she would be thinking more and more of him and dreaming longingly of his assuming his rightful place at the head of the family.

Pressing circumstances might push him aside at the moment, but he would always be close to her heart and Shawn knew human nature well enough to foresee the inevitable reunion. It was an old but true axiom that blood forever ran thicker than the water of friendship, however clear and sweet.

But Theodosia Mallory was in dire need of help, and maybe, just maybe, he could do something toward salvaging her son in the process.

"Like Emmett said, I'm looking for work. If you're sure enough of me to give me a free hand, let me do what I think's right, I'll take over."

"That's it!" Jack said decisively. "Means I'm pulling out."

"No need," Starbuck said. "You probably know this ranch better than anybody else around. You could be a big help."

"Not me. I won't have nothing to do with it while you're running things. I'll leave and

Ballymun Branch Tel. 8421890

after you've busted it up and moved on, then I'll come back." Mallory paused, threw his attention to his mother. "I'm just hoping that when that happens there'll be enough left of Stingaree to put back together!"

Whirling, he started for the door, halted. "I won't be going by myself," he said, shaking a finger at Starbuck. "I'll be taking Rafe with me — him and all his boys. Like as not there'll be some others — all them that figures they don't want to work for a yellow stripe."

Stark muttered something under his breath. Shawn's mouth tightened momentarily, and then he smiled. "I'll consider that a favor. McCoskey'd be the first man on the place I'd fire. You'll be saving me the trouble."

"Well, he sure wouldn't want to stay after he hears what you're aiming to do!" Mallory shouted and moved on.

The front door slammed, banging loud in the early morning hush. Starbuck turned to Mrs. Mallory.

"I'm sorry he feels the way he does."

"It can't be helped, I suppose," she murmured, fingering the folds of her dress. "Perhaps one day he'll realize that there's something more to life than what he saw in his father."

Emmett Stark stepped away from the divan, and hand extended, crossed to Shawn. "Glad you'll be taking over. Want you to know you can count on me for anything."

"Aim to, you and Caleb."

"Just name it, and it'll get done. Know I'm talking up for Caleb when I say that. . . . What's first on the list?"

"The law. The sheriff or the marshal, or whatever you've got around here, has to be told about the murder."

"I don't think it was murder," Theodosia Mallory said quietly. "I believe my husband was shot during that raid and was trying to reach here when he died."

Starbuck studied the woman thoughtfully. Then, "Could be the way of it but it's still something that should be reported. Who's the lawman in town?"

"None in Parsonville. The closest is in Cedar Springs — that's about forty miles away."

"Those men killed when there was trouble before, Pa never reported them," Christine said. "He just had them buried."

"His way of doing it. That's changed now. We go by the real law, not his."

"Whatever you think," Mrs. Mallory said wearily. The strain was at last beginning to show. "I'll send a letter to Cedar Springs."

"Now, about the funeral —"

"There'll not be one — that is, not one in town. We'll hold it here, today. There'll be nobody in attendance except the family and any of the hands who might wish to come. We — we have no friends."

Starbuck made no mention of it but such an arrangement would work to their advantage. The longer the people of the valley were unaware of King Mallory's death, the more time he would have to soothe raw feelings and clear up disagreements. Then he shrugged, having second thoughts on the matter; Jack and McCoskey, and the others who sided with them, would soon, intentionally or not, spread word of the rancher's death, thus defeating that hope.

There was a sudden, quick drumming of hooves in the yard as horses raced away. Mrs. Mallory listened until the sound had died, then turned to Shawn.

"Is there anything you'd like me to do?"

"Nothing special. Go about things as usual, leave the ranch to Emmett and me. We'll get matters cleared up fast as possible and bother you only when it's necessary. I think rest is what you need now. . . . It be all right if I use your husband's office to work from?"

"Of course, and you might as well stay here in the house and take your meals with us."

"Obliged, but it'll be better if I stay with the crew. Can keep a bit closer to things."

"I understand. Will it be all right if Emmett —"

"Up to him," Starbuck replied, noting the hope in Christine's eyes. "Probably a good idea. Ought to have a man in the house at night."

Stark and the girl smiled broadly. Theodosia Mallory said, "There anything else you need?"

"Nothing, just hope you understand I'll have to have a free hand in this. Aim to clear up all the old sores and make restitution if need be. I don't expect to give anything of yours away that rightfully belongs to you, but if a man has a just claim I want to satisfy him."

"It will be hard to determine. King was the only one who really knew what went on. He never talked to any of us about business."

"There'll be papers — deeds and such. Plan to depend on Caleb Fain a great deal, too."

"Caleb — oh yes, the old man who looks after the horses. He went to work for us at the very start."

"Knows most everything there is to know about Stingaree and how it got to be what it is." Starbuck glanced over his shoulder. First light was beginning to break. "Reckon I'd best get busy. Morning's here, and I want to get started."

Mrs. Mallory rose, offered her hand. "I want to thank you, Shawn. I'll be forever in your debt."

"So shall I," Christine said, also rising. "I don't know what we would have done if Emmett hadn't thought of you."

Starbuck shrugged, smiled wryly. "Only hope I can come up to what you're expecting," he said, and nodding to each, turned for the door.

CHAPTER 13

Stepping out into the cool, gray morning Starbuck halted at the foot of the steps that led up to the gallery. Immediately a hunched figure pulled away from the shadows of nearby lilac bushes and the cracked voice of Caleb Fain reached him.

"Was quite a confab. You taking charge?"

Shawn grinned. There was little that got by the old wrangler. "Seems so."

Caleb spat. "Mighty proud to hear that. Place is needing somebody smart to grab hold right quick. What about Jack? Seen him come faunchin' out of there madder'n a tromped-on rattler. Jumped on his horse, then him and Rafe and Milo Green and all the rest of that bunch hightailed it for town."

"Walked out on Mrs. Mallory when she turned the ranch over to me."

"Ought've expected that," Fain said, and glanced up as Emmett Stark came through the doorway and joined them.

Elsewhere the yard was deserted, but lamp-light now glowed in the bunkhouse where the crew was getting ready for the day's

work and in the kitchen as the cook prepared the morning meal.

"Big load off everybody's mind, you
agreeing to stay," Emmett said. " 'Specially
mine."

"Why your'n?" Caleb asked. A change
had come over the older man. He now appeared sullen, disgruntled.

"If Jack and McCoskey'd got their paws
on the place it wouldn't've lasted long, and
I'd sure hate to see that happen to Mrs.
Mallory and Chris. . . . You talked like you
had some kind of a job for me to do,
Shawn."

"You and Caleb both. Going to need
somebody I can depend on. Not fooling
myself that it'll be easy to straighten out all
the trouble King Mallory started. Like for
you to forget your regular chores, hang
around close so's you'll be handy. I'll fix it
with Frank Price."

"He still the ramrod?" Fain wondered.

"He is. Intend to make that clear to the
hired hands. Want the ranch to go right on
same as always, raising cattle. I'll be busy
for a spell calming down Boone Rafferty
and doing chores like that."

"Can sure figure on me to help," Fain
said.

"I'll be needing you when it comes to

clearing up a lot of the deals Mallory made. You know who he skinned, I don't. When I start squaring up with them, I'll be looking to you to tell me whether they're being honest or not."

"That'll be easy."

"Expect I'll find deeds and records in Mallory's office that'll help but they won't tell me all I have to know.

"Emmett, want you to pick about ten men, have them ready to ride soon as they've eaten. Aim to go over to Arrowhead, try to smooth last night over with Rafferty before he takes it in his head to raid us."

"You expecting to run into trouble?"

"Hoping to avoid any but I want the men along for show."

"I savvy. Just want everybody to know Stingaree'll still fight if it has to. What about Jack? You think he'll keep his nose out of it?"

"Not sure what he's likely to do."

"Well, you can quit your guessing," Caleb said. "He'll be trouble. Can bet on him doing everything he can to mess things up for you."

"Not much he can do —"

"He'll figure out something. 'Tween him and Rafe you've got the meanest pair of cusses that ever drawed a breath when it

113

comes to getting back at a man."

The hands were beginning to come from the bunkhouse, yawning, stretching, smoking limply rolled cigarettes as they moved toward the wash house.

"We can handle Jack and McCoskey," Starbuck said. "Least of my worries right now. Important thing is to get over to Rafferty's, head him off before he can do something that'll make matters worse."

"What're you going to do about King — him maybe being murdered, I mean?" Caleb said then. "You just letting it slide?"

Starbuck shook his head. "I'll be doing what I can. Job for a lawman, however —"

"It matter how he got killed?" Stark said. "Mrs. Mallory's satisfied it happened during the raid. Why not let it go at that?"

Shawn gave that thought. Finally, "Got to be sure that was the way of it. If not, it was murder, and whether you or I had any use for Mallory or not, murder is murder and whoever did it can't be left to go free."

"You're taking on a powerful lot of work," Fain observed, shaking his head. "Keeping this place from getting tore to pieces by the wolves that'll start showing up is going to be a big job without you trying to scout out the man that plugged King."

"Already said it wasn't going to be a

114

picnic," Starbuck countered and glanced toward the kitchen. The crew was beginning to file into the low-roofed building. "Let's get some breakfast. Got a few things to say to the help and this'll be a good time."

"Other'n Boone Rafferty, you got plans for the day?" Stark asked as they moved off in the steadily increasing light.

"He's first on the list and the most important. And it could take some time. Expect he'll be hard to talk to."

Entering the dining area, they sat down at the long table, and after all of the crew, including Frank Price, that were to be present, had assembled, Starbuck rose, made the announcements he felt were necessary, and asked that the word be passed on. He stressed the point that Price would continue as foreman. It brought a murmur of approval.

"What about Jack?" one of the riders asked.

"Moved out," Caleb said quickly. "Him and McCoskey and the whole bunch."

"Then he ain't got no say-so on anything?"

"No sir!" Starbuck's running this shebang now. Jack tries to say different, you tell him to go to hell."

Shawn waited until the surge of talking

faded, and continued. "The family will be burying King Mallory today. Any of you want to be there is welcome. Just tell Frank and he'll arrange it."

Only silence followed that, and Starbuck, finished with a hurried meal, rose to leave. Price got to his feet, hastened to intercept.

"Want to say I'm obliged to you," he began.

"For what?"

"Well, things've sort of been going the wrong way for me lately. Kind of expected to get —"

"You're foreman of Stingaree as far as I'm concerned, and you'll keep the job. I'm leaving the bossing of the crew and the raising of the cattle up to you while I tend to other things. If I have any complaints it'll be you I'll do my talking to, not with the men."

Price smiled. "That's the way I was hoping it'd be."

The sudden pound of a horse rushing into the yard and coming to a quick halt brought Starbuck around to the door. A moment later one of the cowhands burst into the room.

"Where's Rafe?" he shouted.

"Not here," Price said. "What's the trouble?"

The man frowned, glanced about uncertainly. Caleb pushed back his chair. "Spit it out, Gabe. McCoskey's done been fired. Starbuck here's running Stingaree now. Do your talking to him."

Gabe swallowed hard, bobbed his head. "Rafe sent me out to the north range. Said I was to keep an eye on Rafferty's, and if they headed this way, I was to let him know fast."

"And?"

"Well, they're coming! Rafferty and about a dozen men — all of them loaded for bear!"

CHAPTER 14

Starbuck swore. Boone Rafferty, vengeance determined, had moved faster than he'd anticipated. He swung to Gabe.

"How long before they'll get here?"

"Fifteen, maybe twenty minutes."

"Cutting across our north range?"

"Not exactly. Following that old wagon road that runs through the grove."

Shawn gave a moment to visualizing the area, faced Stark. "Get those ten men. Got to move fast," he said and then as Emmett turned to the table and began to call out the names of the riders that suited him, nodded to Price.

"I'm borrowing some of your crew. Aimed to tell you before it was necessary but Rafferty —"

"Sure, I understand."

"Couple of other things I want to clear with you but that'll have to wait now until I'm back."

Pivoting, Starbuck headed for the doorway, Caleb, Emmett Stark and the chosen men trotting along behind him. Outside, he veered to the hitchrack where his sorrel waited, mounted, and paused while the remainder of the party claimed their horses at the corral.

"Stark will tell you what's up after we get going," he shouted. "Main thing is we've got to head the Arrowhead bunch off before they get out of the trees."

They swept out of the gate in a tight cluster, Stark behind and to his left, Fain on the right. Shortly the younger man pulled up alongside.

"Just what are we aiming to do — besides heading off Rafferty?" he shouted above the thud of the horses.

"Talk him out of what he's got in mind. Want to do it peaceable if I can."

"He ain't going to be in no humor to listen much."

"Know that. It's the reason we've got some men along. Want you to keep them back, out of sight while I do some explaining. If Rafferty gets stubborn, won't hear me out, I'll signal for you and the boys to show themselves. No more than that — just ride out where you can be seen. Understand?"

Stark nodded. "What if that Arrowhead starts in shooting?"

"I'm figuring they won't but if they do, nothing left other than to fight."

The puncher grinned, dropped back to rejoin the main body of the group. On his right Shawn saw Caleb Fain move in closer. The old wrangler's face was again set and sullen. He didn't look up when he spoke.

"I recollect you saying you had special-like chores for me and Emmett both."

Starbuck glanced at the man as impatience stirred him. Fain was feeling slighted, resented the fact that Stark appeared to be favored. Since he had been on Stingaree longer than anyone else he perhaps had the right to injured feelings, but there was no time for such now. Much depended on dissuading Boone Rafferty from his purpose. Still . . .

"Did, and I meant it," he said, smiling. "Like for you to stay right alongside me, sort of ride shotgun over me. Don't know Rafferty or any of the men who'll be with him."

Caleb bobbed his head. "I'll be right there, case I'm needed," he said, evidently mollified.

"You're acquainted with Rafferty," Shawn continued as they loped on across the grassland. "You figure I've got a chance of talking him out of it?"

The wrangler brushed at his mouth with the back of a hand, pulled at his hat. "Just might work. Boone ain't such a bad sort. Don't see why you're keeping the boys out of sight. Why don't you just meet that Arrowhead bunch head-on?"

"That's what Rafferty would expect from us — a bunch of Stingaree riders spoiling for a fight. But they're my ace if he gets hard-nosed about it."

"Reckon I see what you're driving at. . . . There's that road Gabe was mentioning."

Shawn raised his glance. The faint, dual marks of wagon wheels following a course along the edge of the trees was to their right. The Arrowhead party couldn't be far off, he realized. It was best he get Stark and the men set immediately.

Swinging toward the grove, he continued for a short distance to where the road curved sharply. "In there," he shouted to the puncher, and waved him and the riders into the fringe of the trees.

"You say you've never seen Rafferty?" Fain asked as he and Starbuck pulled to a stop in the open a few paces on beyond and settled down to wait.

"Never."

"Tall, skinny galoot. Ain't much hair between him and heaven but what he's got's kind of sorrel-colored. Talks slow like a Texan, only he ain't. Come from Tennessee same as King, but I reckon you've heard all that. Got them kind of sharp eyes that bore right through a man, and I expect he's a real ringtail when he gets riled, being sort of slow and easygoing otherwise."

"Can figure on him being plenty worked up after last night."

"Ain't misdoubting that. Expect I'd be that way, too, was somebody to come riding into my place shooting and raising hell and burning down my property."

Shawn was scarcely listening. A thin dust cloud was hanging over the trees ahead. The Arrowhead party was not far away. He had no illusions concerning the chance he was taking by meeting the angry rancher and his crew in the open. Since they were on Mallory's land he and Caleb would instantly be recognized as Stingaree men, and shooting could erupt immediately.

He could only hope that their unexpected presence would surprise Rafferty enough to permit his speaking a few quick words before the party reacted wrongly.

"Here they come," Fain warned.

Starbuck saw the first of the horses round a shoulder of brush at the same moment, had a belated thought; he would be a stranger to Rafferty, Caleb was a long-time employee of Mallory's. Alone, he might do better.

"No need for you to stay here. Could wait over there in the trees."

"Ain't about to," Fain growled, mistaking Starbuck's words as concern for his safety. Hitching the pistol on his leg forward to a more available position, he added, "I'll be ready."

Shawn frowned. "No gunplay —"

"I know. I heard what you told Emmett. No shooting unless they start it, but I always figure it's best for a dog to show his teeth so's folks'll know he's got some."

The party had cleared the brush, were coming on. Rafferty was riding a short distance ahead. The rancher raised a hand, as would a cavalry officer, slowed his followers to a walk while he craned to see who the two men before him were and what their purpose might be.

"We're here in peace!" Starbuck shouted.

Rafferty said something to his riders. They spread out, half a dozen to each of his flanks, and then in a line, proceeded. When they were within thirty feet or so he again signaled, this time for a halt.

"What the hell's this all about?" he called sharply.

Shawn, conscious of the hostility with which the Arrowhead men were considering him and Fain, raised both hands, palms forward.

123

"Peace," he said. "Want to talk about it."

Boone Rafferty eased back on his saddle, eyes filled with suspicion. As tension began to mount with each passing second, he said, "Ain't you both from Mallory's?"

"We are. . . . King's dead."

Rafferty frowned as a quick run of talk broke out in the party backing him. After a moment he shrugged.

"Well, I ain't going to say I'm sorry. He got what was coming to him. . . . When'd it happen?"

"Last night. Was during the raid or after. Not sure which."

A hard smile broke the rancher's lips. "You mean he might've got himself a bullet while he was shooting up my place?"

"Could have. Like I said, can't be certain."

A scatter of cheers went up from the Arrowhead riders. From somewhere among them a voice asked, "You hear that, boys? Seems like we winged that old bastard for good!"

Starbuck waited until it was quiet again, then said, "Aimed to ride over and have a talk with you about that raid. Want you to know that things at Stingaree have changed. Mrs. Mallory's taking over. There'll be no more such goings on."

Rafferty continued to smile. "That a fact?" he drawled. "Reckon her and that boy are real sorry for what's been done."

"She is, and —"

"You ain't said yet who you are."

"Name's Starbuck."

"And you was sent to beg my pardon, that it?"

"Something like that. Point is the Mallorys don't want any more trouble — not with you or anybody else. King did a lot of wrong things and they're willing to square up."

"Ain't that easy. Only thing that's going to make me feel better is doing to them what they did to me."

Starbuck shook his head. "Forget it. Not the answer — and you'll have to ride over me to do it."

Rafferty's features hardened. "You figure you can stop me?"

"I'll make a try. . . . Best you listen to reason. I don't say you haven't good cause to feel the way you do, but if you want peace in this valley, you'll call off this raid."

"Don't go yammering at me about peace! That goddammed King —"

"He's dead. Get that straight, Rafferty. You can't do anything to him now. Your vengeance will be wasted if you take it out

125

on his family, and that'd not only be wrong but it would start the fire blazing all over again."

"Then it'll have to blaze," the rancher said doggedly. "Your bunch comes into my place, shoots up some of my men, sets the place afire, and now you got the gall to tell me to forget it. The hell I will! I aim to collect a few licks for what King's done to me."

"No —"

Rafferty spat, raised his hand. "All right, boys, let's get to it — and if them two get in your way, tromp 'em into the ground."

Starbuck half turned, shouted, "Stark!"

Immediately Emmett and the riders with him, guns drawn, and strung out into a line, spurted out of the trees. Surprised, Rafferty jerked his horse to a halt.

"What the hell?" he shouted in a strangled voice. "This here an ambush?"

"Only if you turn it into one," Shawn replied evenly. "We're not looking for trouble, but if you want to go for your guns, we're ready. It's your choice."

CHAPTER 15

Boone Rafferty's eyes narrowed. For a long, hushed minute he studied Starbuck and the Stingaree riders drawn up beyond him, allowing his gaze to drift back and forth over them as he weighed the wisdom of challenge. Finally he shrugged.

"I ain't one for spilling blood. Been a patient man all my life but I came to my limit last night when King and his bunch rode into my place and done what they did."

"He's out of it now," Starbuck said. "Thing to think about is peace."

"Easy for you to say that. You ain't the man who lost a barn and some sheds — and some stock."

"They can be replaced, and will."

The rancher leaned forward. "You mean you'll pay for what I lost in that fire?"

"The Mallorys will."

Rafferty gave that consideration. Then he asked, "Who figures out what'll have to be done?"

"You, long as you're fair and honest about it."

Rafferty settled back, wagged his head. "Well, I'll bet old King's squirming in his box right now if he heard you say that. He never give nobody nothing. All he ever did was shortchange a man after he got done skinning him."

"Like I've said, King Mallory's dead. This is a new deal at Stingaree and the place is going to be run different."

"Hard to believe. . . . Where's Jack fit in this?"

"He's out. All you have to do to show you're agreeable is forget about this raid."

"Reckon I can do that. Not my style, anyway. How do we start the rest of it?"

"Turn your men around, take them home. I'll do the same."

"And the damages?"

"I'll ride into town, tell the storekeeper to give you what you need to rebuild whatever was burned and charge it to Stingaree. Same goes for anything else you lost."

"Had a couple of milk cows and some horses in the barn. Then there was harness and tools —"

"I won't quibble with you about it. Just asking you to be fair."

Rafferty again shook his head, grinned wryly. "Sure is a laugh — Mallory's bunch asking me to be fair! But I get the idea. Not him I'm dealing with now."

"Exactly."

"Well, you can count on me being honest with you. We can forget the tack. Was old and worn out. Aimed to throw it away when I got around to it. Horses were old stock, too. Cows were something else. Good ones, both of them."

"Replace them. The Mallorys will pay the bill. I'll send you horses to take the places of the ones you lost."

"And the lumber and stuff for the barn and sheds, I just get it from Rabinowitz and charge it to you?"

"Best way I know to handle it."

"There won't be no stalling around about it?"

"Rabinowitz, if he's the storekeeper in Parsonville, will get the word today."

Rafferty took a deep breath, smiled as if finally convinced. "Just hard to believe — Stingaree acting like it was human and saying it'll do the right thing by others. Never thought the day'd come."

"It's here," Starbuck said, "and for good. We're not giving anything away and we'll fight if we have to keep what's rightfully the Mallorys'. Want everybody to understand that. What I'm interested in is squaring up old accounts for them."

Shawn roweled the sorrel lightly, moved forward with his hand extended. "You willing to shake on it?"

"I am," Boone Rafferty said, and accepted Starbuck's fingers in a firm grasp.

"By God, that does it!" Caleb Fain said, speaking for the first time. "Reckon thing's'll be mighty different around here from now on."

"No reason for them not to," Starbuck said, and then to Rafferty, added: "Be a fine thing if you'll drop by the ranch and say your sorries to Mrs. Mallory. Know she'll appreciate it — and it'll be a sign that the axe has been buried."

The rancher sobered briefly, nodded. "Reckon I can do that. Never had nothing against her other'n the fact she married a man like King. This evening be all right?"

"Good," Starbuck said, and touching a forefinger to the brim of his hat, wheeled about. "So long."

"So long," Rafferty replied and turned back to his men.

At once Emmett Stark and the Stingaree riders trotted forward, holstering their weapons as they came. Fain, moving in beside Shawn, grinned broadly.

"He done it! He talked old Boone out of it!"

Stark's set features cracked into a smile. "Sure glad to hear that. Mrs. Mallory will be, too. . . . It cost much?"

"What the hell you care?" Caleb snapped, his manner once again changing. "It ain't your money."

"Just some lumber and nails, few hinges and such," Starbuck hastened to say.

"Along with a couple of cows and passel of old broomtails. There's some culls —"

Starbuck shook his head at the wrangler. "Can't afford to pull a slick trick on him now. Horses'll have to be as good as he lost. Worst thing we could do would be to cold-deck Rafferty."

"That's for sure," Stark said, "and we won't. Got plenty of riding stock on the ranch that'll be as good, maybe better'n he lost. Milk cows — that's something else."

"We'll let him find what he wants, then pay the bill. Best way to satisfy him."

"You think the truce'll stick?" one of the riders asked as they moved slowly back toward the ranch.

"Long as we hold to our word," Starbuck replied. "Going to be up to every man working for Stingaree to see that we do."

There was a general nodding of approval to that. Stark said, "Be no sweat there. Ain't a man riding for us that won't be glad it's over with. Can quit looking over his shoulder."

Shawn glanced at Emmett. "Didn't know it had been that bad. Was given to understand that nobody ever dared roust a Stingaree man."

"It ain't been so touchy around here for the last couple of months," Fain said. "Afore that, however, was a different story. Boys had to sort of run in bunches. Never knowed when a fellow going someplace by hisself was liable to get jumped by a sorehead. Was even a few shots taken at us now and then."

Starbuck frowned. The task he'd assumed had a much greater depth of hate than he'd thought. But he should have guessed, King Mallory being what he was.

"Should've been around here a couple of years ago," Caleb continued. "You'd sure got yourself mixed up in some real fireworks — and it'd been the same thing all over again if you hadn't cooled off old Boone."

"There any other big outfit like Arrowhead that we can expect trouble from?"

"Not now. Been too long ago, but you best expect a-plenty from them squatters and three, maybe four little two-bit outfits. Owners of them are still hanging around."

"We'll satisfy them," Shawn said, and

motioned to Stark. "You and the men head back to the ranch. I'll take Caleb and go into town. Want to set things up with that store-keeper."

Emmett nodded, began to veer away with the riders. Caleb grinned admiringly. "Nothing like keeping a wagon rolling once you get it started!" he said. "Now, if we just don't get potshot by Jack and McCoskey while we're going through the woods, every-thing ought to work out fine!"

CHAPTER 16

They encountered no interference from Mallory and his friends and rode into Parsonville around midday. The settlement, no more than half a dozen weather-grayed structures, appeared deserted except for several horses standing slack-hipped at the hitchrack fronting Kottman's Saloon.

"That'll be Jack and Rafe and their bunch," Caleb said, eyeing the mounts critically. "Could figure on them holing up there."

Shawn murmured his agreement and swung his horse up to the general store. Caleb pulled in beside him and they dismounted together, secured their horses, and crossing the wide porch, entered.

Rabinowitz, a squat, dark-faced man with a fixed smile, adjusted his black sateen sleeve guards and came from behind a counter into the center of the well-stocked room.

"It is good to see you, Caleb," he said, and looked questioningly at Shawn.

"Name's Starbuck," the wrangler stated by way of an introduction. "He's took over running Stingaree for Missus Mallory."

The merchant inclined his head sadly. "About King I have heard. A terrible thing. The lady I will soon tell my condolences, when my boy comes to take care of the store."

"You hear about it from Jack?"

Rabinowitz said, "Yes, from him. . . . There is something I can do for you?"

Starbuck outlined his agreement with Rafferty. "Leaving it up to you and him. Expecting you both to treat Mrs. Mallory fair."

"She is a fine lady and my best customer. Also is the Stingaree ranch. I would not cheat the Mallorys. An itemized list will be furnished of all that is bought."

"Think you'll have everything Rafferty will need?" Starbuck asked, glancing about.

"All I am sure. The lumber I can get from the sawmill by dark. I will send my boy with an order of what I believe Mr. Rafferty will want."

"Good. Like to clean up the matter right away. One thing more, if there's anybody else around with a beef against King Mallory, I'd like to hear it."

A smile tugged at the corners of the storekeeper's mouth. "This also I have heard — that you will make good all of King Mallory's — ah — a — transactions. This I did not believe."

"You can," Caleb said flatly. "Starbuck aims to make it up to anybody King skinned."

Rabinowitz nodded slowly. "Such a long time that could take —"

"I'm talking about land," Shawn said. "Can't be all that many men that he squeezed out of the valley."

"It is true, and there are some who have moved away."

"That's the way I see it. Like to see those who still are here. Be obliged to you if you'll pass the word along. Tell them to come out to the ranch." Starbuck paused, then added: "Don't guess you remember me, but I stopped by a time back. Was asking about my brother — if you'd seen him."

Rabinowitz bobbed his head hurriedly. "It is only now I remember you! Your brother, yes. . . . I didn't know you had gone to work for King. . . . You have found nothing of your brother?"

"No. Was wondering if he'd passed through here since I asked."

"A few drifters, yes. Him, no. It is not a main road we are on, but I will watch."

"Appreciate it," Starbuck said, turning away. Disappointment at receiving no word of Ben had long ago lost its sharp edge; he accepted such now as a matter of course.

But something had been accomplished; the arrangement to rebuild Arrowhead's destroyed property was now completed, and only minor items remained.

"You reckon we could spare the time for a drink?" Caleb wondered plaintively as they moved through the doorway onto the porch.

"No reason why not," Shawn answered, and slowed his step.

Ranged in a half circle fronting the store were six men — Jack Mallory, McCoskey, and the riders who had chosen to join them when they departed Stingaree. All had been drinking, with Jack apparently taking the honors.

"Can savvy now why they wasn't laying for us out in the brush," Caleb said quietly.

Shawn resumed his stride, crossed the porch, and stepped down to street level. Halting in front of the line, he folded his arms, faced Mallory.

"Something on your mind?"

"You — damn you!" Jack yelled and jerked out his pistol.

Starbuck's hand swept out, knocked the weapon from the man's grasp, sent it into the dust. Motion to the side caught at the corner of his eye. He pulled back as McCoskey lunged, was a shade slow. Rafe's weight thudded into him with solid force and he went down.

"All of you — just keep back!" he heard Caleb Fain yell warningly as he rolled to his feet.

McCoskey, eyes bright, lips drawn back into a toothy grin, closed in again, both fists swinging. Shawn took a glancing blow on the head, another on the shoulder as he stumbled into Jack Mallory. Swearing, he pivoted, came squarely about. Throwing up his left arm, he blocked another swinging right of McCoskey's, stalled the gunman in his tracks with a hard right to the jaw.

Rafe rocked on his heels, shook his head as if to throw off the effects, and came on. Starbuck, twisting and turning as he tried to free himself of Mallory's clawing hands dragging at his shoulders, stabbed McCoskey in the eyes with a knuckled left, crossed with a right.

The gunman howled a curse. "Get a hold of him, goddammit! Grab him by the arms!"

Dust, churned up by scuffling boots, was beginning to hang in a brown-gray cloud in the street. Two men had come out of Kottman's, were watching from the landing. Rabinowitz had also been drawn into the open by the sounds of the encounter and was standing in front of his door, features strained and anxious.

Starbuck, weary from being up at so early

an hour, sweaty and low on patience, freed himself of Mallory with a quick whirl to one side. Instantly he swung on McCoskey. He jabbed the gunman with his left, turned him half around, nailed him with a solid right — and staggered forward as Mallory flung himself upon his back.

Instantly McCoskey bored in, taking full advantage of the moment. He brought an uppercut from his heels, barely missed with it as Shawn jerked his head to one side. Moving fast, he followed with a second blow that caught the tall rider on the ear.

Seething, but remembering old Hiram Starbuck's admonition never to lose his temper at such moments, Shawn threw himself to the left. Mallory, caught off guard, twisted partly around, slackened his grasp. Starbuck locked on the man's wrist with one hand, his hair with the other, and bracing himself with spread legs, buckled forward.

Mallory yelled in pain, fought to keep his balance as he rocked uncertainly on his feet. Still holding the man's wrist, Shawn whirled, swung him hard into Rafe McCoskey. The gunman swore wildly as they came together and both went down in a dust-raising tangle of legs, arms, and bodies.

Instantly Starbuck moved in on them. Grabbing McCoskey's collar, he pulled the man to his knees, drove a balled fist mercilessly into his jaw. As Rafe fell away, Shawn reached for Mallory, caught him in a viselike grip with his left hand, smashed him on the chin with his right.

With both men sprawled in the street, Starbuck stepped back, sucking hard for wind. He flung a glance at the other riders. They were watching silently, hands raised under the steady aim of Caleb Fain's pistol.

"Pick 'em up!" he snarled. "Get 'em out of here!"

Milo Green and the one they called Tuck started forward, paused, looked questioningly at the wrangler and his menacing weapon. It was evident that neither wanted any misunderstanding at that moment.

"You heard him!" Caleb said, lowering his gun slightly. "And when they come to, be telling them they'd best stay out of sight."

Shawn leaned against the corner post of Rabinowitz's porch. Wadding his neckerchief, he mopped at the sweat and dust caked on his face and blurring his eyes, and watched the punchers drag McCoskey and Jack Mallory to their feet.

"Don't be toting them over to

140

Kottman's," Fain warned. "That's where me and my partner are headed."

Milo Green slowed his step. "Then where the hell —"

"Morgan's barn," Caleb replied, waving his pistol at a bulky, long-abandoned structure at the end of the street. "It's good enough for them two."

Mallory was stirring weakly. McCoskey, however, supported on both sides by two of his friends, still hung limply between them as they moved off through the thinning haze.

The old wrangler holstered his six-gun, swung his satisfaction-filled eyes to Shawn. "Now, about that there drink —"

Starbuck ruefully touched the side of his face where Rafe McCoskey had landed a solid blow. "Can use one," he said, and pulled away from the porch.

CHAPTER 17

The word spread quickly. That next day, near midafternoon, as Starbuck sat at King Mallory's desk checking through a leather folder containing deeds and other papers pertinent to the ranch, two men rode in and asked to see him.

Matters were proceeding smoothly at Stingaree. There had been nothing more heard from Jack and his friends, although Mrs. Mallory did inquire about her son when Shawn made his report to her on the deal he'd made with Boone Rafferty. King Mallory had been laid to rest, Frank Price had resumed his proper stance as foreman, and all hands had settled down to the ordinary business of raising cattle. He was well along the way to clearing up Stingaree's problems, Shawn thought; the job wasn't proving to be as difficult as he'd anticipated.

The first of the two claimants, a small, thin man named Woodson, had owned property adjoining the ranch on the west.

"Was a nice little farm," he declared belligerently. "Was doing fine, then Mallory comes along and tells me flat out he wants my land."

"You get paid for it?" Starbuck asked, glancing at Caleb Fain sitting across the office from him.

"Ain't saying I didn't, but I was cheated. Never got half what the place was worth."

Caleb shifted on his chair, wagged his head. "Now Ira, you know that ain't true. Sure King said he could use your land, but you come to him first saying you wanted to sell. Can recollect just what you said because I was with him."

"Well, I —"

"You told him you was sick to death of farming and that you could see now that it wasn't fit for growing but only for cattle, and you wanted to quit."

Woodson thrust his hands into the pockets of his stained trousers, shrugged. "Well, maybe it was something like that, but I should've got more money."

"King give you what you paid for the land, seems."

"Didn't get nothing for the house I had on it."

"House! Ira, that weren't no more'n a lean-to, and you damn well know it! Couldn't even be used for a line shack, it was so poor. King had the boys go over and burn the whole shebang soon's you'd moved off."

Woodson made no comment. Starbuck, locating the quitclaim among Mallory's papers, scanned it briefly.

"Appears to me you were treated fair," he said. "You wanted to sell. Mallory gave you what you'd paid for the place."

" 'Cepting that he hankered to own everything in the valley, I don't know why King bought it anyway," Caleb said. "Sure wasn't no use to him."

Shawn tucked the deed back into the folder. "Nothing I can do for you."

Anger flared through Woodson. "Can see you're going to be just like old King — beating folks out of their just dues same as he done! Way I heard it you was aiming to make up for all the mean tricks he pulled, but you ain't no different. Just all talk —"

"Simmer down, Ira," Fain said quietly. "Why don't you just own up to it that you're trying to do a little skinning yourself? You heard what Starbuck here's trying to do for Missus Mallory and you figured you'd try grabbing onto a few dollars more for that hardscrabble cabbage patch you was so happy to get shed of. Ain't that the real truth?"

Woodson looked down. "Was only

144

hoping to get fair pay for what was mine."

"You got it," the old man said, "so you might as well forget trying to hornswoggle the Mallorys out of any more."

Woodson turned away, moved toward the door. He hesitated there for a moment, then with a resigned twist of his shoulders stepped out into the yard.

Caleb grinned. "Reckon we can't fault a man for trying."

"Guess not," Shawn agreed. "Probably have a few more just like him. Reason I want you around. Need you to help me separate the sheep from the goats."

The old wrangler dug into his jacket, produced a blackened pipe and a doeskin pouch of tobacco, sank deeper into his chair. "Well, I can't think of nobody King didn't pay something to. Maybe he scared them into selling, things like that, but he always forked over the hard cash. The argufying comes from whether it was enough or not."

Emmett Stark appeared, halted, stood framed in the doorway. "That jasper that was just here," he said, frowning. "Rode off cussing us good. Said he aimed to get even with Stingaree."

"Had no claim," Shawn explained.

Stark scratched at his jaw doubtfully. "I

— I don't know. He must've felt he had a call coming. Maybe we ought to take care of him anyway — just to keep everything peaceable and going right."

Shawn considered the puncher in silence. Caleb was not the only one who had changed. Whereas the old wrangler seemed to withdraw into a shell of resentment in the presence of Emmett, the rider was assuming an air of authority where the ranch was concerned. Recalling the fact that he and Christine Mallory planned to marry, Starbuck supposed it was only natural. But until Theodosia Mallory herself relieved him of his duties he would continue to exercise his own judgment — the approval of Stark notwithstanding.

"A man comes here with a just claim, he'll get satisfaction," Shawn said. "The ones trying to swindle us will get turned down."

"And that's what Ira Woodson was up to," Caleb said, seemingly enjoying the moment. "Far as him stirring up any trouble, he ain't got get-up enough to holler sooey if the hogs was rooting him."

Stark's mouth tightened. "Have it your way," he said stiffly, and glanced over his shoulder. "Here comes another one."

Caleb rose, looked out into the sunlight-flooded yard. "Henry Carr. Was squatting

146

on a place down at the south part of the range. Good spring there and King figured he needed it for a water hole."

Shawn flipped through the deeds, located one signed by Carr. . . . One hundred and sixty acres — one hundred and sixty dollars.

"The water all that was worth anything?"

Fain shrugged. "Oh, expect Henry was doing all right. Water's about all a man needs in this country to make a farm grow, but it wasn't no great shakes of a place."

The wrangler hushed and Stark drew back as steps sounded on the landing outside King Mallory's office. Carr entered, a gray, leathery man with stolid features.

"You Mr. Starbuck?" he asked, ignoring the other men and fixing his small, sharp eyes on Shawn.

Starbuck nodded. "What can I do for you?"

"Name's Henry Carr. Caleb there knows me. Had a farm down a ways and King Mallory come and took it away from me. When I heard he was dead and that you was looking to make things right with them that he robbed, I decided I'd come talk to you."

Shawn picked up the deed, held it so that Carr might see the signature. "You sign this?"

"My name and writing sure enough. Ain't denying that."

"Then what's the problem?"

"Problem's that I plain didn't want to sell. Told King that three, four times. Was just me and my old woman and we was getting along fine on the place. Had most all we wanted and couldn't see no reason to give it up.

"But King, he wouldn't take no for a answer. Kept deviling me. Then one night a bunch of his men rode their horses through my corn and vegetable garden. Tromped everything into the ground. Next day King showed up with that there paper for me to sign. Flang me eight double eagles and said for me to put my name on it and move.

"Well, way things was, my crop lost and me not being young no more and him crowding me the way he was, I figured I'd best do what he wanted. So I signed and moved."

Shawn glanced at Caleb for confirmation. The wrangler nodded.

"Now, I didn't come here begging," Carr continued. "I could've stayed put, I reckon, and maybe King would've give up and let me alone, and maybe he wouldn't. I sure don't know, but I don't feel like I got a square deal."

"You think you ought to have more money?"

"Nope, I'd like to have my place back. Me

148

and my woman ain't done no good since we was drove off. Money he give me didn't last long and I can't hold no job nowhere. Man my age don't get work so easy. Figured if I could have my farm back, I could maybe get on my feet again."

Starbuck mulled the problem about. One hundred and sixty acres, even though it had a spring on it, was a small parcel of ground where Stingaree was concerned — and there was plenty of water available elsewhere for the cattle.

"You agreeable to paying back the money Mallory gave you for the land?"

"Sure," Carr said, scuffing the floor with the toe of his run-down boots, "only I ain't got it. Do have a few dollars but it'll take them to buy seed and vittles so's I can get started again."

Starbuck reached for a blank sheet of paper and a pen, wrote out a promissory note for the hundred and sixty dollars. Shoving the paper toward Carr and handing him the pen, he said, "All right, you get your place back but you'll have to sign a note for the money Mallory paid you."

The older man grabbed the pen eagerly, hesitated. "I ain't sure when I can pay — and that's a fair lot of money."

"No time limit on it. You make it next

year, fine. If not, pay Mrs. Mallory what you can. She'll be reasonable about it."

Carr scratched his name on the note, laid down the pen, and stepped back. "Hard to say how much I'm thanking you," he mumbled.

Shawn nodded, folded the sheet of paper, and placing it with the deed, tucked them back into the folder. "You'll get all of your papers when the note's paid."

"Yessir, I understand. It be all right for me to start working the farm now — or maybe tomorrow?"

"Up to you. It's your property."

Carr, beaming happily, thanked him again, bobbed his head to Fain and Emmett Stark, and departed.

Caleb struck a match to his pipe, sucked it into life. Between puffs he said, "Was the thing to do but there'll be some hollering about losing that water hole. Only one in that section of the range."

"Plenty of water in the river. If we're needing a place there, take a team of horses and a fresno and dig a ditch, make one."

"Hell a-mighty!" Fain exclaimed, startled. "It'd have to be a mile long!"

Shawn smiled. "What's easier — drifting cattle to the other places or digging a ditch to replace Carr's?"

Caleb snorted. "Knowing cowhands, I'll say they'll stick to driving the cattle."

"Still might be a good idea," Stark said. "Reckon we ought to do some thinking on it."

Shawn leaned back in his chair. Not even a full day had passed as yet and already the minutes were beginning to drag. Sitting behind a desk, sifting through dry, legal documents and listening to the complaints of others, was not his idea of enjoyable work. In the saddle and on the move was more to his liking, but he'd agreed to take over for Theodosia Mallory, get matters at Stingaree straightened out, and he'd not go back on his word.

"You got another'n," Stark said, glancing into the yard.

Shawn sighed, reached for the leather folder. "Who is it this time?"

"Boone Rafferty," Emmett replied.

CHAPTER 18

Rafferty rode slowly into the yard, the two hands with him keeping a short distance behind. He'd not thought it necessary for them to accompany him, but Ed Fowler, his foreman, had insisted. Ed, like the rest of the Arrowhead crew, put little trust in the turnabout that was supposed to be taking place at Stingaree.

It was the first time in many years he had come to the Mallory house, and idly glancing about he took note of the few changes that had been made. King was never one to blow much money on improvements, he recalled, preferring instead to lay the cash aside or invest it in something that would bring a return. His building such a fine house had been somewhat a surprise when it occurred, but thinking on it later he'd come to the conclusion that Mallory had erected it more as a symbol of himself rather than as a grand home for his family.

He didn't begrudge King its presence, however; actually he was glad of it for it made Theodosia's life more pleasant and God knew she'd had little enough of the good and gentle things life offered.

Starbuck. . . . That was the fellow's name. . . . He'd see him first, then go pay his respects to Theodosia. At once Rafferty swung the bay he was riding toward the east end of the big house where King had maintained an office. As he drew near he caught sight of a tall puncher standing in the doorway — Emmett, Ed Fowler had called him — and beyond him at King's desk, speared by the late afternoon sun shining through a window, Starbuck.

"Set easy," he said to the pair trailing him as he drew to a halt. "Ain't figuring on being here long."

Dismounting, he draped the leathers of the bay over the hitchrack, absently gave them a tug, and stepped up to the doorway. Emmett nodded to him, friendly enough, and drew back to let him pass. He entered the shadowy room, seeing then a third man slumped in a chair near a corner, nodded. It was Caleb Fain, who'd been around since the day when he and King had started ranching. He'd always felt it was his tough luck that Caleb had chosen to work for Mallory instead of taking the job he'd offered, but King was one who always somehow ended up with the best.

Starbuck, smiling, looked up from where he sat. "Evenin'."

Why the hell couldn't he ever find a man like this Starbuck to hire, he wondered bitterly. All that ever came to his place looking for a job were the culls, the ordinarys, the average.

"Evenin'," he replied, brushing at the sweat collected on his forehead. "Been a hot one."

"Has at that."

Starbuck was a hard one. A man could see it in his eyes — sort of cool gray, almost like steel. And the way he'd handled himself in town with Jack Mallory and that bastard, McCoskey, proved it wasn't just looks. Rabinowitz said he'd mopped up the street with them — taking on both of them at the same time.

"Just wanted to say I rode in, talked with Sol Rabinowitz. Told me you'd been there already, had fixed it for me to get whatever I needed to build my barn."

"That was our deal."

"Know that." Rafferty paused, suddenly embarrassed by the realization he was making it sound as if he had doubted Starbuck's promise and had gone to the scorekeeper for verification. Down deep in his mind he supposed there was some truth in it. "Was wanting mainly to see if Sol had everything I'd be needing."

"Told me he'd have it all and that he'd get word to the sawmill —"

"He did," Rafferty said. "First load of lumber's coming in the morning."

"Good."

"Made up a list for you, the one you wanted of the stock I lost. Got it right here."

Starbuck reached for the slip of paper, glanced at it, passed it to Emmett. "Leaving it up to you to see what's named here gets sent over to Arrowhead — tomorrow."

Emmett said, "Sure," and put the paper in his pocket.

"You found the cows you wanted yet?"

Rafferty grinned. Starbuck wasn't one of those to conveniently forget. "Nope, not yet. Ain't had time to go looking." He paused, reset his hat. "Reckon that about covers it. Thought I'd drop over to the house, offer Mrs. Mallory my sympathy like you mentioned. You figure it'll be all right, it being this time of day and all?"

"Be fine. . . . Like to ask you a question. During the raid, did you happen to see King while it was all going on?"

Rafferty thought back. He'd been in the yard almost from the moment when one of the hands had yelled fire and had stayed there until it was all over.

"Nope, come to think of it, I sure didn't.

Remember seeing Jack and Rafe McCoskey and some I don't know, but not King. Guess he was waiting off to the side somewhere."

"Could be," Starbuck said.

"Reminds me of something I almost forgot. Seen Jack in town, him and McCoskey, couple others. The two of them was a little worse for wear, but I reckon you know all about that.

"What I want to say is they come up to me when I was leaving. Told me not to get too set on things, that it wasn't over with yet. Guess you could say they was threatening me."

"Not much I can do about them," Starbuck said. "Jack pulled out, took McCoskey and his crowd with him. They've got nothing to do with this ranch."

"Jack's a Mallory, ain't he?"

"Yes, but he's got no say-so now. His mother gave him a choice, he picked leaving, turned over the place to her."

"I see. Well, whatever, wanted you to know that Jack's likely up to something, and I'm holding Stingaree responsible —"

"Don't. Anything he does is on his own. Has no connection to this ranch."

Boone Rafferty shrugged, moved for the door. "Maybe so, but far as I'm concerned, he's still a Mallory."

Maybe it wasn't exactly fair to lay Jack off onto Starbuck's shoulders, Rafferty admitted, but he couldn't see any other way around it. Somebody had to put a halter on Jack; he wouldn't let what was happening at Stingaree pass without trying to put a stop to it. He was like King that way — had that same mean streak.

"Just keep waiting here," he said, motioning at his two riders. "Won't be more'n a couple of more minutes."

He wished now he'd not listened to Fowler, had come alone instead. Both of the men were dog-tired, and hanging around in Stingaree's yard made them uneasy. . . . He'd cut his visit with Theodosia short, for their sake.

Reaching the steps to the house, he moved up to the front door, and pulling off his hat, knocked. Almost at once Christine answered the summons. He took a deep breath. The girl was the spitting image of her mother twenty-five years ago.

"Your ma — I'd like to see her for a moment," he said hesitantly.

"Of course, Mr. Rafferty. Won't you come in?"

He didn't expect the girl to remember him, but then she had grown up, undoubtedly did a lot of riding and had seen him somewhere.

Stepping by her, he entered the house, halted in the foyer. Christine disappeared behind one of the doors to his right, and shortly Theodosia, looking cool and reserved and beautiful as ever in a dark-blue dress, came forward, hand extended, to greet him.

"Boone," she murmured. "So nice of you to drop by."

He took her slim, warm fingers into his own, pressed them lightly. "Just wanted to say I was sorry."

She had changed little since he had last seen her despite the sort of life she'd found with King. The same dusky loveliness, the same deep blue eyes and red-brown hair that always seemed to glow when the sunlight struck it.

"It was a shock," she said, and then added, "I'm forgetting my manners. Won't you come in and sit for a few minutes?"

He shook his head. It was best not to tarry — best for him and likely for her. "Need to get back to my ranch. Just wanted to tell you I was sorry, and have a word with your man Starbuck."

Theodosia smiled. "I was pleased when he told me that arrangements had been made to repay your losses. I — I hope that an end has come to all the trouble we've seen in the valley."

"It's here if he keeps doing the way he is. I run into Henry Carr on my way back from town. Told me Starbuck had give him back his place. All he had to do was sign a note for what King paid him for it. That kind of treatment's going to make friends for you again."

"I know it — and I hope it makes us friends again, Boone."

"Reckon you and me were never anything else but. It was King I —"

"He's dead and buried and no part of things now."

"Of course. Up to me to forget. Well, I got a couple of cowhands out there getting saddlesores waiting for me. Besides, it's growing on toward supper time."

"You will come again?" Theodosia asked hopefully as he moved for the door.

"If you say."

"I do, Boone. . . . I've missed you."

"Same goes for me — and it was all a pot of foolishness! King had no call to get jealous and climb up on his high horse the way he did. From the day back in Greenville when you two got married, I figured it quits far as you and me were concerned. Aimed to be nothing more than a family friend."

"He could never let himself believe that. To outsiders he was always a hard, strong man, sure of himself, but that wasn't entirely true. King had doubts, the same as other people, and the biggest was about you and me."

"For no reason — and because of it a lot of years have gone to waste," Rafferty said, shaking his head. After a moment he smiled. "Maybe we can start making them up. . . . Good night."

He heard her reply as he crossed to the gallery's edge and descended to the yard, her voice stirring him just as it had from the beginning almost thirty years ago. Thirty years — had it only been that long since King took Theo away from him and made her his wife? It seemed more like twice that.

CHAPTER 19

"The whole blamed thing's just plain going too good," Caleb Fain said that next morning as they sat at their early meal. "Ain't natural."

Starbuck drained the last of the coffee in his cup. "Had that feeling myself. There a chance we've seen the end of trouble?"

"No, sir, not when you're dealing with the likes of Jack Mallory and Rafe McCoskey! They ain't about to forget it."

"Yeh, him jumping Rafferty yesterday proves that. Could've been mostly talk, however. Left out like Jack is, he's bound to be plenty sore. . . . Reckon we'll have any more visitors with a gripe, like Carr and Woodson?"

The old wrangler gave that deep consideration. "Could be a couple or so. Ain't many still around. If you'd started doing this a month from now you'd probably had Lockridge and Huckaby and a couple others to fuss with. King was all set to take them over." Fain paused, looked closely at Shawn. "You getting fiddlefooted?"

Starbuck stirred. "Can think of plenty of

things I'd rather be doing. Never been much of a hand to work from a chair."

"Reckon I know what you mean. Was that way myself when I was a younker. Aiming to quit?"

"Told Mrs. Mallory I'd stick until it was all cleared up. I'm leaving it to her to say when."

"That might not be too long seeing as how Stark's worming himself in so good with her. Living in the house it's like he's a regular member of the family."

"Probably a good idea. Ought to have a man in there. Anyway, he and Christine are planning to get married. That happens, he'll be a member of the family and can sort of take over, fill Jack's place."

Caleb was silent for a full minute, then asked, "They for sure getting hitched?"

"What I heard Mrs. Mallory say."

"Well, I ain't so sure she's helping things much. Misdoubt he's big enough to take hold, run this ranch."

Shawn pushed back his chair, rose. "With you and Frank Price to give him a hand he ought —"

"Best folks don't figure too strong on me," Fain cut in, also coming to his feet. "Could be I won't be around."

"You thinking about pulling out?"

Caleb's thick shoulders stirred. "Maybe. Been around here for a long time — longer'n anybody 'cepting the Mallorys themselves. Man can wear out his welcome, seems."

Shawn sighed wearily, crossed to the doorway, and stepped down into the yard. The crew had already ridden out to begin the day's work, relieving the men who had been on night herd and were now beginning to trickle in, anxious to get their breakfasts and crawl onto their bunks.

"It on account of Emmett that you're feeling that way?" Starbuck asked, facing the older man.

"Ain't grudging him or nobody else what he can get for himself. Man don't make the most of what comes his way, he's going to find himself left out."

It was the reason, of course, Shawn knew. Caleb was the senior employee of the Mallorys and he had come to resent Emmett Stark and the opportunity that was being presented the younger man. Likely, down deep, Fain felt the same about him.

"Hate to hear this," he said. "Your being here's worth a-plenty to me — and I expect it is to Mrs. Mallory, too."

"She'll have Stark," Caleb replied gruffly and looked off toward the east where the sun was beginning to break over the horizon.

"Here he comes now. Expect he had a fine night, sleeping in a soft bed in a private room, taking his vittles with the womenfolks."

Shawn remained silent. Fain was in no mood to be prodded. Best to let it ride, hope to smooth over his ruffled feelings later. Perhaps he could think up more important duties for the oldster, give him some authority that would bolster his injured pride. . . . He'd do a bit of studying on it.

"Mornin', gents," Stark greeted cheerfully as he came up. "Sure looks like a fine day."

"Reckon it is — for some," Fain muttered, reaching for his pipe.

Stark frowned, shrugged, turned his attention to Shawn. "Mrs. Mallory told me to thank you for the way you're doing things. She was right pleased yesterday when Boone Rafferty dropped by. Said it was like old times talking to him and that she owed his being there to you."

"Likely would've come by without me mentioning it to him."

"And that deal you made with Carr —"

"How'd she know about that?"

"I told her," Stark said. "Didn't you want me to?"

"Don't see any reason to bother her with things like that."

"Well, she wants to be. Feels she needs to know everything that's going on around here if she's to keep Stingaree running."

"Ain't no need for her to fret, not with you taking charge," Caleb said caustically, and pivoting, moved off across the yard for the bunkhouse.

Emmett watched the older man leave, a puzzled light in his eyes. "What's that mean?"

"Never mind. . . . Everything all right at the house?"

"Sure is," the puncher replied, and then hesitated. "You done any more thinking about King — about him maybe not getting himself shot accidental-like, but bush-whacked instead?"

"Some. Haven't had much chance, however. Did talk to one of the crew that was in on the raid — one of those that didn't pull out with Jack. Said he thought he saw Mallory at Arrowhead, but he wasn't sure. There was a lot of dust and smoke."

"Then most likely he got shot there."

"Would make it possible. Couple more men I aim to talk to about it."

"Mrs. Mallory's still satisfied that it was an accident. Far as she's concerned you can leave it at that."

Shawn nodded. He had given that consideration earlier. It would be easier just to drop the whole thing, but the thought of doing so disturbed him. If there was a killer running loose, others of the Mallory family could be in danger; besides, letting a murderer go unpunished was wrong, went against the grain.

"Letting it go would be easy. Only problem is I might find it hard to sleep at night. . . . Mrs. Mallory come right out and say she wanted me to forget it?"

"Not exactly, but I sort've got that feeling."

It seemed odd to Starbuck. You'd think a man's widow would want to be certain, and if there was a killer on the loose, want him to be brought to justice. King Mallory was different from most men, however, he had to admit that. And because he had been the source of so much trouble and ill will, it could be that Theodosia Mallory felt it best to let the affair slide off into oblivion.

"There anything special you're wanting me to do today?" Stark asked.

Shawn shook his head. "Can't think of anything other than sticking around in case there's trouble."

"Which ain't likely. Chris and me — we figured to take a picnic lunch and ride over the ranch. Some parts of it I ain't ever seen,

166

and she's been on every foot of it. Got some favorite places she wants me to see."

There could be some danger in such, Starbuck thought. If there was a killer around bent on taking revenge on the entire Mallory family, they would be needlessly exposing the girl. . . . But he had no proof of the possibility.

Stark misunderstood his hesitation. "Mrs. Mallory's all for it — sort of thinks it's a good idea."

Shawn smiled faintly. "Go ahead, but keep wearing your gun and watch sharp."

"Why?"

"McCoskey — and Jack."

"Hell! Her own brother — he wouldn't hurt . . ."

Maybe not, but Rafe and his bunch don't listen to him — he listens to them. . . . And there could be others."

Stark pulled off his hat, ran fingers through his shock of hair. "Guess you're right, and I'll keep my eyes open," he said, and turning, headed back for the house. "See you later."

Shawn followed slowly, angling off toward Mallory's office at the end of the structure. Sitting down at the desk he again busied himself with the rancher's papers, thumbing through them with little enthusiasm. There were at least six more one-time residents who could be expected to post a complaint judging from the ridiculously low price paid them for their holdings.

But the day dragged by without any of them putting in an appearance, which he decided was just as well since Caleb Fain had also failed to present himself and take his usual counseling position in the corner. No one had seen him since early morning, Shawn learned on inquiry.

Near mid-afternoon he saddled the sorrel and rode out onto the range in search of the wrangler, taking advantage of the excursion to talk with two more of the party who had been on the raid at Arrowhead. Neither was of much help; they had not noticed King Mallory, both declaring they had been too busy.

He ranged farther than he had intended, wrapped in thoughts of Mallory's possible murder, the problems of Stingaree, and his desire to finish the job and resume the way of life he preferred, so he was late in returning to the ranch. Most of the hands had already had their supper and he took his meal alone, eating quickly and indifferently at the end of the table.

Shortly after finishing, as he was walking toward Mallory's office in the deepening shadows, the fast pound of a running horse and the slice of iron-tired wheels cutting into the sandy soil brought him around. Moments later a buggy whirled into the yard, swerved up to where he stood. Sol Rabinowitz was hunched forward on the seat, face flushed with alarm.

"It is bad news — bad news I've got for you!" the storekeeper shouted, scrambling off the vehicle.

Shawn stiffened. "What is it?"

"McCoskey and Jack — they go to Boone Rafferty's to again burn his ranch!"

CHAPTER 20

Seizing the arm of the highly agitated merchant, Shawn shook him roughly. "You know that for sure?"

Rabinowitz bobbed his head wildly. "Yes, yes, yes! Two drifters they hire come to my store for bullets. I hear them talk of what they will do."

Starbuck swore. Not only would the raid undo all he'd accomplished in removing the stain besmirching the Mallory name in the Gila Valley, but it would rekindle the warfare he had succeeded in arresting. This time there would be no halting a bloody conflict; Rafferty had made it clear that regardless of momentary circumstances, Jack Mallory was still Stingaree.

"How long ago did they pull out?"

"Already they had gone when I hitched my buggy and came to warn you."

That meant the raiding party was by then near Arrowhead — possibly even there. Starbuck swung his attention to the members of the crew that were gathering around, attracted by the hurried sound of the arriving buggy. His jaw hardened, seeing neither Stark nor Fain.

"Anybody know where Caleb is — or Emmett?"

"Ain't seen 'em all day," one of the men replied. Others gave the same answer.

Temper stirred Shawn. When he needed the pair most one was off on a lark, the other sulking somewhere unknown. Frank Price stepped forward.

"You want me and the boys to help?"

"Best you all stay here. I'm going to Rafferty's, try to warn him ahead of time. If I'm late it could be he'll bring his bunch, pay us back in kind."

"Hell, he knows Rafe and Jack ain't Stingaree no more," one of the riders protested.

"Way he looks at it a Mallory's still a Mallory. One of you get my horse." Shawn faced Rabinowitz. "Obliged to you. It won't be forgotten."

The merchant, calm now, nodded slowly. "It was for peace that I had hope, now it is already gone. . . . There is something more I can do?"

"Nothing," Starbuck replied and turned to meet the cowhand bringing up the sorrel. Swinging onto the saddle, he threw his glance to Price. "Keep every man you've got on watch — and post guards."

Roweling the gelding, he sent the big horse thundering across the hardpack. Midway motion on the porch of the ranchhouse drew his attention. Theodosia Mallory was standing at the top step. He could not distinguish her features in the half dark but undoubtedly she was wondering at the excitement.

He touched the brim of his hat with a forefinger, raced on toward the gate. She should be made aware of the new crisis, of course, but he could not take the time to do so. Like as not Rabinowitz or Frank Price would do the chore for him.

It never occurred to him until he was away from the yard and cutting across the range that the woman could have wanted to speak with him about her daughter and Emmett Stark, that she, too, shared the fear that something could have happened to them — a thought that was growing stronger in his mind now with each receding moment. He should have heeded his very first consideration of the possibility, not permitted his anger at Emmett's inopportune absence and the pressing need to move quickly wash it from him. He should have directed Frank Price to mount a party, go in search —

Starbuck shook off his feeling of blame.

Stark was no greenhorn. He could take care of the girl and himself, and if there had been trouble somewhere on the range, surely one of the crew would have known of it. The men rode far each day and he doubted there was any part of Stingaree that was not touched.

Crouched low, he continued to press the sorrel for speed. It was risky, he knew; with darkness now closing about the country, the footing was becoming increasingly dangerous. But he had to take the chance. Jack and McCoskey had a long start on him.

He glanced ahead. Arrowhead was still miles in the distance and the certainty began to grow within him that his hope of reaching Rafferty's before Mallory and the others was in vain. He did have a shorter route, slicing directly across the range from Stingaree while Jack and his party had the extra distance from town to cover, but even so, with the start the raiding party had, only a miracle would get him there ahead of them.

He didn't like to think of the consequences if he arrived too late. Boone Rafferty would listen to no excuses, accept no explanations. As far as he'd be concerned, the war between his Arrowhead and Mallory's Stingaree, stayed only by a stroke of luck a few days before, was underway once again. And this time it would not end until both ranches were in charred shambles and much blood had been shed.

The gray-green grass, the long, gentle slopes, the rounded ridges, continued to flash by under the driving hooves of the sorrel. The air was cool, thanks to high-hanging clouds carrying the promise of rain, and now and then a bird, frightened by the gelding's passage, whirred off into the darkness.

He should be drawing near — three quarters of the way, at least, Starbuck thought, again raising his eyes and straining to see the country beyond. He was not too familiar with that part of Stingaree's range, and spotted nothing that evoked any landmark recollection within him. Now was when he would find Caleb Fain's presence of help; the old wrangler would know exactly where they were, could advise him as to the best approach —

A tightness gripped Starbuck's throat. Far ahead, an orange-colored glow was mounting into the dark sky, faint now but deepening steadily. It could only be Arrowhead. He was too late. It had already been put to the torch.

He swore helplessly. In spite of all his efforts they were back where they had started. The war was on just as if it had never been stopped — and all because of Jack Mallory and Rafe McCoskey. . . . He should've done something about them that day in Parsonville when he had the chance. But what? He couldn't just shoot them down, and there was no local jail into which he could demand they be locked for safekeeping.

Grim, he raced on through the night, gaze now fixed on the flaring red hanging over the land. There was little he could do now but press on, reach Arrowhead, and there seek out Boone Rafferty and try to explain. He held small hopes of a hearing, however.

He began to slow the gelding's headlong pace. The faint popping of guns, well in the distance, drew his attention. He frowned, trying to isolate the sound, place its location. Arrowhead was directly north, the reports seemed to be coming from the east.

Starbuck rode on, still puzzled by the meaning. Abruptly he crested a ridge, looked down on the ranch. The main house was swathed in roaring flames. Farther over he could see sheds, corrals, even the stack of recently acquired lumber for the new barn, dwindling into glowing embers. The job of burning down Arrowhead was thorough this time. By morning there would be nothing left standing.

He could see men hurrying about, running from what was apparently a horse trough to the ranchhouse, vainly struggling to control the flames with buckets of water. It was useless. The leaping flames were having their way and nothing could check them.

Again he heard the distant crackle of guns, now much farther to the east. Understanding came to him. Jack and McCoskey, with their followers, had been driven off, were now being pursued.

It had to be done, regardless of personal danger. He'd tried to prevent such a thing, had failed. Now he must see Rafferty, talk to him, make him see that Stingaree was in no way to blame.

Squaring himself on the saddle, Starbuck touched the sorrel with his rowels, rode down the slope to the flat where the ranch lay. Stiffly erect, tense, noting several wounded men and a body or two lying about the yard, he walked the gelding toward the trough, the center of activity, and halted.

After a brief time his presence was noted. The men, realizing the hopelessness of their efforts and glad for the opportunity to stop, dropped their buckets and turned to him. All were blackened from soot and smoke. Most showed burned places in the clothing and on their skin where live sparks had fallen and found purchase. In the eerie, yellow haze they looked unreal.

"He's one of them!" a voice yelled suddenly. "Blast the sonofabitch off his saddle!"

CHAPTER 21

Starbuck's hand swept up. The round muzzle of his forty-five centered on a squat, square-faced man directly in front of him.

"You're dead if anybody tries it," he said coldly.

The puncher was motionless for a long breath and then he shrugged. "Hold your fire!" he yelled above the dry popping of the flames.

Starbuck nodded. "That's better. Now, what do they call you?"

"Name's Ed Fowler. I'm ramrod for this outfit."

"All right, Fowler. I came here to talk to Rafferty. Where is he?"

Arrowhead's foreman glanced about at the men gathered around him, brought his heat-reddened eyes back to Shawn.

"What about?"

"Want him to know this raid was no doings of Stingaree."

"Like hell! Was Jack Mallory and that bastard of a McCoskey leading the bunch."

"They were on their own. Made that clear to Rafferty last night. Call him."

"Don't reckon he'd hear," Fowler said, and pointed to one of the bodies sprawled in the yard.

Starbuck swung off the sorrel, a tightness again closing in on his throat. Holstering his pistol, he crossed to where Rafferty lay. The rancher had been shot in the chest, likely died instantly. He turned slowly, heavily.

"Saying I'm sorry about this —" he began, and stopped. Fowler and the Arrowhead men had moved in behind him, now faced him in a solid, threatening circle. Beyond them other members of the crew battling smaller fires elsewhere in the yard were abandoning their chore and coming in to see what was taking place.

Starbuck studied the men coolly. "Forget it," he said. "There's been enough killing for one night, and cutting me down won't help any."

"Help a-plenty, you goddammed, doublecrossin' —"

Shawn shifted his attention to the puncher, a small, elderly man. "You've got it wrong, mister! Stingaree had nothing to do with this. Neither did I. Peace had been made and —"

"Was the Mallorys that broke it!"

"Jack Mallory — not the Mallorys."

"All the same far as we're concerned."

Shawn swore. "It's that kind of dumb thinking that keeps a feud going!" he snapped. "Now, I'm sorry about Rafferty. Mrs. Mallory'll feel the same, but you can't blame his killing on anybody but Jack and Rafe McCoskey."

"Was Rafe that shot Boone down."

Starbuck fixed his eyes on the speaker. "You saying he didn't get hit during the raid?"

"Nope, was after things was about over. I was standing over there by the tool shed. Boone was doing something near that load of lumber. I heard somebody yell his name and looked around. It was that damned McCoskey. Then he just ups and shoots Boone and turns around and takes off. I hollered at some of the boys who was getting their horses, told them, and they lit out after Rafe and the others."

"They'll catch them, too," the elderly puncher said. "Come morning, them that ain't shot full of holes will be swinging from the trees."

A lynch mob. . . . Starbuck turned toward his horse. Regardless of what Jack Mallory and the others had done, a lynching was not the answer. It was the law's job to deal with them.

"Where you think you're going?"

At the harsh question Shawn halted, came about. Fowler was leveling his pistol at him. The rest of the crew, hands resting on their weapons, stood ready to back him.

"That lynching's got to be stopped. Aim to try."

"You ain't doing nothing!" the old cowhand shouted. "You're staying right here and maybe getting the same thing!"

"Stringing up's what Jack Mallory's got coming, and what he's going to get!" another voice declared.

"Maybe, but I don't hold with murder, and that's what it will be," Shawn said. "Leave it up to the law. You've got a witness that saw McCoskey shoot down Boone. Let the law hang him. It'll take care of the others, too, if you'll give it a chance."

"Ain't no law around here — and we don't figure to wait. We're squaring up for the killing that's been done here tonight, and for Boone's sake, we're squaring up with Stingaree. Owe him that much."

Starbuck's anxiety deepened. "Stingaree?"

"Time we get through with it," Fowler said, "it'll look like this place. . . . Take this bird over and tie him to that tree 'til we decide what to do with him, a couple of you. Then get ready to ride."

Two men stepped up to Starbuck, seized

him by the arms and escorted him roughly to a large cottonwood at the edge of the hardpack. Backing him against its thick trunk, the younger of the pair pulled his six-gun from its holster, thrust it under his own belt.

"Get some rope," he said to his companion.

The puncher glanced about, halted his eyes on Starbuck's sorrel and the coil of rope hanging from the saddle.

"We'll just use his'n," he said, and led the gelding in close.

Shawn watched narrowly as the rider freed the coil and began to shake it out. The man guarding him waited impatiently while elsewhere in the yard, partly obscured by the hanging smoke and darkness, the remaining men prepared to make their vengeance raid on Stingaree.

"Come on, come on —"

He had to risk escape. Once they got that rope around him, bound him to the tree, he'd be helpless to do anything — even if they permitted him to live. The realization flashed through Starbuck's mind, brought a tenseness to his long body.

He placed his attention on the rider before him. Weapon leveled, hammer cocked, it would be suicide to make any sudden move; the man needed only the slightest reason to pull the trigger. . . . Best he hold off until they started to put the rope around him. His chance might come then.

The Arrowhead rider stepped in close, rope held between his two hands as he sought to place it across Shawn's chest and wind it around the cottonwood. Arms raised in obedience to the weapon pointed at him, Starbuck gathered his muscles. This would be his one opportunity, his one hope.

He waited. The man with the rope leaned against him, endeavoring to bring the strands together. Instantly Starbuck locked his hands together into a club, brought them down with all the force he could muster. The blow caught the rider on the back of his neck. As he sagged forward Shawn threw his weight against him, drove him into the man with the ready pistol. Both went down in a tangled heap.

Starbuck stepped quickly to the struggling men. Bending low he snatched his pistol from the belt of the squirming, cursing rider on the bottom of the pile, wheeled to the nervous sorrel standing close-by, and vaulted onto the saddle.

"Hey — he's getting away!"

Shawn didn't know which of the two shouted the warning. Likely the one who had been holding the gun on him, since the other was probably still groggy from the hammerlike blow he'd taken. . . . He could care less. All that mattered was getting clear of the smoldering remains of Boone Rafferty's ranch and stopping the lynchings.

CHAPTER 22

A splatter of gunshots racketed through the night. Starbuck, hunched low over the gelding, heard the clip of bullets tearing through the leaves of rabbitbush and other tall growth into which he was spurring his horse. He could not be seen, he knew, and the men could only guess at his location. He had only to fear a lucky shot.

The gate opening into the yard was suddenly before him. Still low, he rushed the sorrel through it, began the climb to the crest of a slope. The shooting ceased. He turned his head, listened for the pound of pursuing riders. He could hear nothing, and when he reached the summit of the grade he realized the Arrowhead men were not giving chase; likely they had decided to forget him and get on with the raid, believing he'd be too late to halt the lynchings anyway.

The firing he'd heard earlier when approaching Rafferty's had been to the east of the ranch. He was on a well-traveled road, he saw, and at once concluded it was one used by Arrowhead in journeying to and from town. Logically, Mallory and the men with him had been fleeing toward the settlement with the Arrowhead posse following.

He would have to accept that, regardless; there were now no pistol shots to guide him and it was both impractical and impossible, because of the darkness, to search for signs. He would simply have to gamble, stay on it all of the way into Parsonville, keeping a sharp watch for any activity to the sides, and hope that he was right.

It occurred to him as the sorrel began to stretch out over the deep-cut, dusty trails that perhaps he should have ignored the plight of Mallory and McCoskey, let them fend for themselves. His first obligation was to Theodosia Mallory and Stingaree, now about to feel the impact of a devastating raid by Rafferty's men. Maybe he should have returned, sounded a warning, and made preparations to ward off the attackers.

But Arrowhead would not catch Stingaree napping. He'd cautioned them before riding out and put Frank Price in charge. They would be ready and Rafferty's crew, seeking retaliation for the sake of the dead rancher, would not find the going easy.

Besides, Jack was, after all, the son of Theodosia Mallory. His responsibility, whether he liked to admit it or not, extended to include him under such circumstances just as it embraced Christine. If Jack died at the end of a lynch mob's rope, how could he tell the woman that he had chosen to protect the ranch in preference to going to the aid of her son? It would be difficult to justify his decision to her, and as for his own conscience, it was something that would haunt him forever.

Starbuck broke through his thoughts, listened into the night, straining to hear above the steady drumming of the sorrel's hooves. His ears had picked up the distant, hollow crackle of guns on ahead. He continued to listen. The sounds did not come again. He relaxed. It could have been some other noise, or perhaps he'd only imagined it.

Shortly he topped out a pine-covered ride. A broad valley, indistinct under the cloud-masked stars, lay below him, and winking faintly in the blackness were several lights. . . . Parsonville, at last. Starbuck muttered his relief, and crouching lower on the saddle, called upon the big gelding for greater speed.

They swept down the long grade at a reckless pace. Assuming he was right in believing Mallory and his friends, pursued by the Arrowhead men, had ridden for the safety of the settlement, he could still be arriving too late to prevent the lynchings. If he'd guessed wrong, and the chase had not ended in the town, then he certainly was too late. He'd have no idea where to search for the party, and Jack and the others would have to meet their fate without any possibility of help.

He reached the foot of the slope. The sorrel, breathing hard, stumbled a little as his front hooves met the level ground, recovered, and raced on. He could no longer see the lights, but the road was definite, would lead direct into the town, and he had no fear of bypassing the settlement.

Abruptly gunshots flatted through the night, this time crisp and definite, leaving no doubt as to their authenticity. Shawn, feeling tension crawling over him, stared ahead. The chase had ended in Parsonville, that was clear, also. Apparently Mallory, with Rafe McCoskey and whoever else had been with them on the Arrowhead raid, had holed up in one of the few buildings, and Rafferty's men were endeavoring to drive them out. . . . If true, there was still time to beat the rope.

He was right, Shawn saw, as he slowed to a halt at the end of the street. A dozen or so horses were standing about, abandoned. Here and there dark shadows moved cau-

tiously as they converged on a bulking structure at the edge of the settlement. . . .
Morgan's barn, he recalled Caleb had called
it — an old, deserted livery stable. Jack and
the others had taken refuge inside.

"Let's rush 'em!"

At the cry, the night erupted with the
crash of guns. The crouching figures surged
forward, raced toward the sagging, totally
black building.

CHAPTER 23

Shawn spurred the sorrel in behind a lean-to near the barn. The charging men gained the building. The shooting increased and then ceased abruptly.

"Get a light, somebody!" a voice yelled.

Boot heels pounded in the street as one of the party hurried across to Kottman's, rapped again when the man returned, the lantern in his hand bobbing up and down in the darkness as he ran. Arrowhead had succeeded in overwhelming Mallory and the others holed up with him in the barn. The lynchings would follow.

Grim, Starbuck tied the sorrel to the makeshift shelter and moved forward quickly to the corner of the barn. The staggering doors were partly shut and he could see nothing of what was taking place inside. Drawing his pistol, he crossed the width of the weathered structure, halted at its opening.

"Throw them ropes up there — over that rafter. . . . And bring me that barrel. They can stand on it."

"Now, wait — you can't do this!" It was

Jack Mallory. His tone was pleading, protesting.

"The hell we can't! You and your bunch've been asking for this a long time. We aim to oblige you."

"Be doing folks around here a favor, too."

Shawn pressed in close to the narrowed entrance. Removing his hat, he peered around the edge. There were seven Arrowhead men. They were gathered in a circle around Mallory, Rafe McCoskey, Mr. Green, and two strangers. Either Jack's raiding party had been fewer in number than he expected, or some had escaped during the fight into town.

The lantern that had been hung on a nail in one of the roof supports now threw its glow down onto the taut features of the five men lined up shoulder to shoulder while their hands were being lashed together behind them. Two of Rafferty's crew were holding ropes slung across an overhead beam, another was settling the barrel called for into place beneath it. Others, weapons ready, watched in silence.

Starbuck glanced around the stable, calculated his chances for stopping the lynchings. The Arrowhead men were too widely separated for his single gun to cover, and the seven-to-one odds were not good to think about — at least for the moment.

"Aim to be real nice to you," the husky, swarthy-skinned rider who seemed to be in charge of the posse said, reaching for Mallory's arm. "Going to let you be the first one to swing."

Jack yelled, jerked away. Two men blocked him, shoved him back into the center of the circle. A third dropped a noose around his neck, pulled it tight.

"Get him up there!" the squat puncher ordered, pointing at the barrel.

Mallory began to kick and twist as he struggled to break free. He was sobbing loudly, promising everything, anything, but his words fell on deaf ears. The pair handling him boosted him up onto the small, circular platform of the barrel's end, held him while the rope was anchored to one of the end posts on a nearby stall. That done, both stepped back.

"Reckon he's all set, Tully," the taller of the two said, nodding at the husky man.

Shawn flicked a glance to McCoskey and the other victims. Rafe appeared unmoved, almost uninterested in the proceedings and what awaited him. A man who had long walked in the shadows outside the law, he likely expected such as an ending to his life one day and thus accepted it now with fatalistic stoicism. Milo Green was also motion-less, but his features were drawn, reflecting the fear that gripped him.

It was different with the two drifters. Both were working feverishly at freeing their hands while all the time claiming they were guilty of nothing more than accepting a proffered job, the nature of which they were unaware of.

No one was listening to their protests. Boone Rafferty's men had fallen silent now that the moment of death was before them, and were staring woodenly up at Mallory. Jack's eyes were closed. His lips moved slowly.

"All right, let's get this over with!" Tully barked. "We got four to go." Folding his arms, he raised his glance to Mallory. "You're getting a choice. You can jump or we'll kick the barrel out from under you. What'll it be?"

There would be no better time than these moments when attention was focused on Mallory. Hand gripping his pistol, Starbuck slipped quietly through the doorway and ducked into the first stall. . . . He waited for reaction. None came. He had not been noticed. Taking a deep breath, he stepped out into the runway, faded into the dark depths of the adjoining compartment.

"Say what you're wanting!" Tully shouted at Mallory. "We ain't got all night!"

He was as close as he would get without attracting attention, Shawn realized. Bracing himself, he stepped into the wide runway and in three long strides reached the edge of the lantern's flare.

"Stand away from that barrel!" he snapped.

The Arrowhead men wheeled as one. A pistol blasted, filling the old barn with deafening echoes. Starbuck heard the bullet thud into the thick timbers behind him, fired hastily at the rider who had reacted. The man jolted, clutched at his leg, and stumbled back.

The place was in instant, utter confusion. McCoskey and the three waiting to take their place on the upended cask were suddenly alive, lunging into their captors as they sought to distract them, knock them out of the way. Powder smoke was drifting lazily about, mixing with the dust stirred up by scuffling feet.

Starbuck rushed to the post where the rope encircling Mallory's neck was anchored, jerked the tag end, released the slipknot. If anyone had collided accidentally with the barrel, overturned it, the hanging of Jack Mallory would have been an accomplished fact.

Lashing out with his pistol at a rider crowding in on him, Shawn crossed to where Mallory yet stood.

"Jump!" he shouted.

Jack appeared paralyzed, but Starbuck's harsh command seemed to jar him into reality. He leaped to the dirt floor of the barn and, off-balance, rocked into one of Rafferty's party, sent him to his knees. Another gunshot ripped the haze. A man cursed in pain, but Shawn, crouched, digging into his boot for the knife he carried there while striving to keep moving all the while, could not tell who had been hit; one of the drifters, he believed.

The choking dust and smoke was working in his favor. Coupled with such close quarters, the Arrowhead men were reluctant to use their weapons, fearing to shoot one of their own. . . . The knife came free of its scabbard. Starbuck crowded in close to Mallory, slashed the rawhide cords that bound his wrists.

"Cut the others loose!" he yelled, and staggered as a fist came out of nowhere and caught him flush on the jaw.

Reeling back, he came up against the side of a stall, steadied himself as the puncher pressed in. It was Tully.

"Might of knowed it'd be you!" he shouted, and swung wildly.

Shawn blocked the blow with his left arm, struck Tully alongside the head with his pistol, turned to ward off another man coming at him from the left. He stalled him with a stiff-armed left, raised his leg, and planting a foot in the puncher's belly, shoved him back into the milling, grunting fray.

McCoskey was free of his bonds. Shawn had a glimpse of the gunman as he smashed a blow into one of the Rafferty men's face, saw him wrench the gun from the rider's hand, and then, as the fellow began to fall away, jam the barrel of the weapon against his body and pull the trigger.

As the thundering echoes of the shot filled the barn, McCoskey lunged toward the runway, bowling over several who blocked his path. Starbuck rushed forward to halt the man. His intent had been to save the gunman from a lynching, but only so the law could take its course.

"Rafe!" he yelled.

In the next instant he was going down, tripped by one of the sprawling punchers on the floor. He had a fleeting look at McCoskey leaping over him, racing along the runway. Twisting about, he snapped a bullet at the man, missed. An instant later Rafe had plunged through the doorway and disappeared into the darkness.

CHAPTER 24

"Damn you — you turned him loose!" Tully snarled. "He's getting away!"

"Not yet," Starbuck answered, and sprang upright.

Gun in hand, he ran to the opening, darted into the night. Rounding the corner of the barn, he legged it for the street where he had seen the horses. Almost to the end of the building's wall, he heard the quick hammer of hooves. A moment later the blurred silhouette of a man crouched low on the saddle and flogging his mount unmercifully rushed up in the darkness. . . . Rafe. . . . He was heading south, hoping to put distance between himself and the town — the Gila Valley and the crimes he had committed.

"McCoskey!"

Shawn stepped into the open as he shouted the man's name. Rafe fired instantly, evidently expecting interference and having his weapon ready. The bullet whipped by Starbuck as he took aim, pressed off a shot. McCoskey threw up his arms, lurched sideways on his horse, and fell to the ground.

Shawn stood motionless looking down at the crumpled figure, almost at his feet. Lamps were showing in the windows of buildings along the street and a few of the braver souls had now come into the open, but they were keeping their distance.

Taut with an anger born of frustration, Starbuck locked his fingers onto McCoskey's collar and dragged the outlaw back into the circle of light in the old barn.

"You wanted him dead — here he is!" he snapped, releasing his hold. "This enough killing to suit you?"

Mallory, Milo Green, and the two drifters had drawn back against the wall of the runway. Milo had managed to get his hands on a pistol, was keeping the Arrowhead riders at uneasy bay. One of the drifters had wrapped a bandana about the wound he had in his leg. The Rafferty man McCoskey had killed lay nearby.

Tully shook his head. "Had it coming to him. He shot Boone — in cold blood."

"Not saying he didn't, but it was up to the law to make him pay, not you. . . . Now, this is all over with. I want all of you to mount up, go back to Arrowhead."

"What about them?" the puncher asked, pointing at Mallory and the men lined up with him.

"I'm taking them with me, to Stingaree. Sent for a lawman a couple of days ago. Likely there by now. I'll be turning them over to him."

Tully's lips curled. "Maybe. . . . Who give you the say-so around here, anyway?"

"Nobody. I took it," Starbuck replied coldly. "And I don't want any trouble from you — any of you."

The Arrowhead man continued to glare at Shawn for several moments, and then he looked down. "Reckon you're right, there's been enough killing. Too much — and if you say you'll see that these birds gets what's coming to them —"

"That'll be up to the law. Far as I can see, everybody's guilty around here — you as much as they —"

"Was them that murdered Boone! Some of our other boys got shot down, too."

"Applies to Stingaree. They lost some men, same as Arrowhead did. And King Mallory was killed."

"Was Rafe that done it," Milo said quietly.

Everyone turned to Green in surprise. Jack caught at the puncher's arm.

"No — he wouldn't shoot Pa!"

"Was him, all right, and I ain't saying it just because Rafe's dead. Ain't got no reason to." Milo paused, looked at Mallory. "Done it on account of you."

"Me!" Jack said in a strangled voice. "I didn't know anything —"

"Was for you just the same. Rafe figured with King out of the way you'd take over the ranch and he'd have himself a real soft job, specially after he got rid of Rafferty, too."

Mallory shook his head. "Me and Pa never got along. I'll admit that, but I wouldn't have nothing to do with getting him killed."

"Could be you're telling the truth," Shawn said. "Nobody but you knows for sure and that makes it your problem. If you're not, it's a lie you'll have to live with the rest of your life."

"It's the truth, so help me!" Jack said desperately. "I didn't know Rafe was going to do it."

"Folks'll find it hard to believe. You and McCoskey were plenty close, and you did a lot of listening to him."

"Know that, and I see I was wrong. Got my eyes opened, aim to keep them open if I can have the chance."

"Between you and the law," Starbuck said, and turned his attention to Tully. "You through talking?"

The Arrowhead man shrugged. "Guess

so. . . . Can't see no use going back to Rafferty's. Nothing left of the place."

"Somebody's going to have to look after the stock until the court settles things. Thing for all of you to do is get back on the job. You'll draw your pay just the same."

Tully glanced at the men with him, bobbed his head. "Hadn't thought of that," he said. "Except we'd best be getting back. Couple of you pick up Nate. We'll bury him in Boone's graveyard."

As the Arrowhead men started to move out, Tully thrust forth his hand. "Friends?"

"Friends," Starbuck said, "and let's keep it that way. You need any help, come to Stingaree for it."

"We'll sure do that," the puncher said.

If there still is a Stingaree, Shawn thought as the riders moved by him for the door. The rest of Rafferty's men, by that time, would have struck the Mallory ranch. The raid could still be in progress. He had purposely avoided any mention of it, and apparently the possibility had not entered the minds of Tully and the other Arrowhead punchers.

"Got to get back to the place fast," he said when the last Arrowhead man had disappeared into the night. "Fowler was getting set to lead a raid on Stingaree when I left

202

Rafferty's. I warned Price to be on the watch for it, but he could be needing help."

Mallory snatched up his gun from the floor where it had been tossed. "Let's get moving then."

"Count me in, too," Milo Green said, "if you want me."

The two drifters exchanged glances. "Us too."

Shawn nodded, easily reading their thoughts. Any assistance they gave would be taken into consideration and be a help to their cause. He doubted it would count for much where the law was concerned, but it did solve the immediate problem of getting them back to the ranch with no difficulty.

"Good enough," he said, "long as you savvy there's no strings attached."

CHAPTER 25

"Don't hear no shooting," Milo Green said as they swung into the small side valley that led to the ranch.

"Ain't no sign of fire either," Mallory added.

Starbuck made no comment, hesitating as yet to draw any conclusions, but he was feeling better. There should be a glow in the sky if Ed Fowler and his raiding party had succeeded in putting the torch to the place.

Shortly they broke into the open and the ranch lay before them. Lights were blazing in the windows and there was no indication of trouble. Shawn breathed easier. Frank Price had evidently been able to hold off Rafferty's vengeful crew.

They pounded through the wide gate, swept by the main house and into the yard, drew to a halt. Well over a dozen men were sitting or squatting in a small cluster in front of the bunkhouse. Around them were an equal number of Stingaree riders. All were holding rifles or pistols. Frank Price came forward at once.

"We caught 'em," he said, eyeing Green

and the two drifters suspiciously. "Got the whole push corralled and waiting for you."

Starbuck swung off the sorrel, walked to where the soot-smudged Arrowhead men had been assembled. From the tail of his vision he saw Jack Mallory pull away, walk his mount toward the house where his mother and sister were standing on the porch. A man was at the girl's side. Emmett Stark, he assumed. Again relief ran through him.

Halting before Rafferty's sullen crew, he said, "Trouble's all over. You're free to go."

Price turned to him, frowning. "You turning them loose? They come here to burn the place down. If we hadn't been all set —"

"What were you figuring on — an execution?" Starbuck countered drily. "Want everybody to understand this — it's finished. McCoskey's dead and there'll be no more fighting or raiding."

Ed Fowler rose from the center of the Arrowhead riders. "What happened to the rest of my boys?"

"On their way back to Rafferty's. I'll tell you the same as I told them — somebody's got to run the ranch until the court settles things. They agreed. Up to you to do the same."

Fowler nodded slowly, pointed at Milo Green and the two drifters. "What about them — and Jack Mallory?"

"We'll let the law decide."

The foreman shrugged. "Reckon everybody's sort of to blame." Turning, he glanced at the men behind him. "Let's get cracking. Going to be a lot of work to do."

The riders began to move off toward a cluster of horses tied up at one of the corrals. Price said, "You want me to lock these birds up?"

"Whatever you think. Just so they're here when the marshal comes," Shawn replied wearily and headed for the cook shack. It had been a long, hard day, and most of a night; he was not only dog-tired but hungry as well.

"Reckon I ought to be telling you I'm sorry."

At the sound of Caleb Fain's raspy voice, Starbuck paused, faced about. The old wrangler moved up to him from the side of the bunkhouse.

"Forget it," he said. He could have used some help both at Rafferty's and later at Parsonville but there was no use in talking about it now.

"Was off acting like a danged fool, mooning around and feeling like I was

206

passed up. Then I got a hold of myself and come back. You was gone and all hell was getting ready to bust loose.

"Was just about to go chasing after you when Missus Mallory came looking for me. Asked for me, nobody else. Said she was worried about the gal and Emmett, wanted me to go hunting for them. Figured I knew the ranch better'n anybody else since I been here so long." The note of pride in Caleb's voice heightened. "Said if anybody could find them it'd be me."

"Can see she was right," Shawn said, ducking his head at the figures on the porch.

"Weren't no big job," Fain declared expansively. "They wasn't lost, or in no kind of trouble. They'd took off for Cedar Springs, got themselves hitched."

"That's good," Starbuck murmured.

With Stark now a member of the family, and Jack straightened out and coming to his senses — not to mention the fact that Caleb Fain had overcome his peeve — the end of his job as the head of Stingaree was in sight.

"Sure do hope I didn't cause you no big trouble," the wrangler said. "But I reckon it was all for the best."

"Probably was. . . . How about having a cup of coffee with me?"

Caleb rubbed at his jaw. "You go ahead,

I'll come later. Right now I'm going up to the house, see if there's anything else the missus wants me to do."

"That's a good idea," Shawn said, smiling, and continued on across the now deserted yard for the kitchen. Reaching there, he halted, looked back over his shoulder.

The Mallorys and Stark no longer were on the porch and Fain was a shambling figure mounting the steps. Rafferty's men had ridden out, and Frank Price and his prisoners, as well as the Stingaree crew members who had been present earlier, had all disappeared inside the buildings. Everything had quieted down — finally.

"Damon? Damon Friend?" a voice called softly from the darkness alongside the cook's quarters.

CHAPTER 26

Shawn stiffened. A tenseness gripped him as he searched the shadows next the low-roofed building.

"Don't know what you're up to, old hoss, calling yourself Starbuck, but howsomever I reckon it's purely your business."

"Step out in the light so I can see who you are," Shawn said tautly.

"Hell, Damon, it's Jake Wiser," the voice replied. "We was working for the same outfit down Wickenburg way a spell back. Thought you looked familiar when you rode in to Rafferty's — I been punching cows there the last couple of months — but there was so damned much smoke and dust I didn't get no good look. But a bit ago when you was telling Ed and us boys to head back, I got me a closer squint."

There was a squeaking of leather and then the thunk of boot heels moving along the side of the cook shack as the man dismounted and came forward.

Abruptly Wiser stepped into view, a burly, hard-faced man, streaked with soot, clothing burned in many places. There was

209

a raw-looking place on his left forearm where a burning brand had left its mark. He halted a stride away from Shawn, stared, and then the wide grin on his lips faded.

"Hell, you ain't Damon Friend, are you?"

"He's my brother," Starbuck said. "I've heard we pretty much look alike."

"But you're calling yourself Starbuck —"

"My name. His, too. Changed it to Friend when he left home. . . . I've been hunting him."

Wiser's attitude altered perceptibly. "What for?"

"Our pa died, left a pretty fair amount of money in the bank to us. Can't be touched, however, until I find Ben — that's his real name — and take him back so's the estate can be settled."

The man relaxed. "I see —"

"Where'd you see Ben last?"

"Arizona. Was a couple or three months ago. We was working for a mining outfit near Wickenburg. He still is, far as I know."

Shawn heaved a long sigh. . . . A direct line on Ben's whereabouts once more. Arizona, and Wickenburg, weren't very far distant; this time he just might get there before it was too late.

"Obliged to you for the information," he said, thrusting out a hand to Wiser. "When I see Ben I'll tell him I talked with you."

The puncher nodded. "Just say howdy for me. You aiming to head out that way soon?"

Shawn glanced toward the house. The windows of the parlor still glowed with light. The Mallorys, reunited and reinforced now by Emmett Stark's entrance into the clan, were probably laying their plans for Stingaree and the days and years to come. They wouldn't need him.

"Tomorrow maybe, or the next day at the latest. Obliged to you again. . . . So long."

"So long," Wiser echoed quietly, and turned back to his horse.

We hope you have enjoyed this Large Print book. Other Thorndike Press or Chivers Press Large Print books are available at your library or directly from the publishers.

For more information about current and upcoming titles, please call or write, without obligation, to:

Thorndike Press
P.O. Box 159
Thorndike, Maine 04986 USA
Tel. (800) 223-1244 or (800) 223-6121

OR

Chivers Press Limited
Windsor Bridge Road
Bath BA2 3AX
England
Tel. (0225) 335336

All our Large Print titles are designed for easy reading, and all our books are made to last.